The Earth Fights Back

Colin Diyen

Langaa Research & Publishing CIG
Mankon, Bamenda

Publisher:
Langaa RPCIG
Langaa *Research & Publishing Common Initiative Group*
P.O. Box 902 Mankon
Bamenda
North West Region
Cameroon
Langaagrp@gmail.com
www.langaa-rpcig.net

Distributed in and outside North America
by African Books Collective
orders@africanbookscollective.com
www.africanbookcollective.com

ISBN: 9956-579-22-X

It is not easy to take a book right to the end when you are still trying your hand at writing, and that is why I abandoned *The Earth in Peril* half way. To be honest with you, it was not easy. Actually, I had always wondered how chaps like Chinua Achebe managed to sit down and come out with very entertaining pieces of literature. My first attempt to write anything had been far from successful. After scribbling a few words, I was fogged. It did not flow the way I thought it would. I had given up and made up my mind to remain a reader, rather than struggling to become a writer. I was therefore compelled to enjoy what other blokes had succeeded in putting in writing. All the same, apart from Bernard Shaw, Giovani Guereski, Tom Sharpe and Wodehouse, I could not come to enjoy much else.

It was not until I started developing insomnia that I discovered that I could use that period of sleeplessness to make another attempt at becoming an author, and be listed among the famous writers. When I had mentioned this to my dear wife, Gladys, she had laughed derisively and asked, "What are you going to write about, politics or your uneventful biography?"

"None of that" I had replied. "You know I have never been a serious man, so I cannot write anything serious. I will think of the beginning of a story and write anything that comes to my mind."

Gladys had laughed a little more and said, "I only hope you will not become the laughing stock of the year."

I would have given up if I had not been a tough egg. Brutus accused Caesar of being very ambitious, when he was groping for a plausible reason for having murdered the emperor. I think I can safely say in this case that I am a lot more ambitious. I therefore went ahead to put pen to paper every time I had insomnia, and succeeded in coming up with *The Earth in Peril.* I hope you enjoyed it the way Gladys Diyen did when she finally decided to read it. What had finally convinced me however, that my book was worth reading were the positive remarks from a very concerned sister, Marceline Sangle Abonga, who said she was always confident that I could work wonders.

Maybe I would have stopped there but for the fact that Bertrand, Kini Maya, Nange and Momjang, my wonderful bambinos whom I had employed as my proof readers because they were cheaper and more efficient, declared that they would not see me abandon a good book midway. They even went ahead to give me very useful hints that enabled me come out with *The Earth Fights Back.* I hope you will find it equally interesting, that is if you found *The Earth in Peril* interesting.

I must admit the great role of Kola coffee. Never allow yourself to be defeated by sleep or tiredness when there is Kola coffee to boost you up, especially when it is brewed and served by a very concerned sister. Yes, Martha Naya Genevieve Ndam made sure my coffee was always there to dissuade me from shirking work on this novel under the lazy excuse that I was tired or sleepy. Aah, Kola coffee!

Gladys is now aware that she did not marry a lazy bum but a Master, who could successfully run the Daily Show over CNN.

The memory of Isidore Irvine Diyen will always inspire me and I will never fail him.

PROLOGUE

Awobua, the king of a small rocky satellite of Mars, known as Mungongoh, had a life's goal, and this was to rid the earth of all humans and transfer his subjects to the earth. All the top brains in Mungongoh had thus been concentrated in an institution meant for the development of ideas to conquer the earth, popularly known as the IRDI or Institute of Research for the Development of Ideas. This institution had surfaced with various diabolic ideas, hideous enough to make Lucifer jealous that he was not the author, but which apart from causing much sorrow on earth had never actually proved efficient enough to rid the earth of all mankind. They had introduced plagues, Bird and swine flue, Ebola, HIV/AIDS and many others. They had even introduced a weapon of mass destruction, the neutron bomb, and would have completely cleared the earth of humans if their plans had worked as intended.

The king had regularly taken out his frustrations on his servant dwarfs, who were generally the ones in the way when his fists went flying. Apart from being used as side stools, the dwarfs served the king's favourite drink, *mukal* when ever he ordered for it. Mobuh, his flabby chief minister was his main liaison with the people of Mungongoh and paid total allegiance to him. He equally succeeded in getting the life of Professor Itoff, the head of the IRDI, spared by King Awobua after several failures by the IRDI, to produce results. Other prominent members of the IRDI, were Dr. Funkuin, Fulumfuchong and Yivissi.

Non members of the IRDI worth noting were; Ngess, a simple man who had the ability to assess correctly and deduce the right outcome, but just like Cassandra in ancient Troy, his opinion, was always sought only after a seemingly impeccable idea had failed; Nyamfuka, a handsome spy attached to Dr. Funkuin.

King Awobua kept ferocious lions as pets, and the mangled bodies of dwarfs that he often hammered to death by his vicious outbursts of anger were provided as choice tit bits to the lions. Mungongoh citizens that were suspected of treason equally ended up here. A few of the members of the IRDI blamed for having failed to provide the king with the opportunity of taking over the earth, also met with death through the champing jaws of the lions.

The last great idea developed by the IRDI was a massive offensive against the earth, and this involved the use of every pestilence available and the neutron bomb. To achieve this, agents were dispatched in their numbers to the earth to smuggle out and take to Mungongoh, every material or item that would be used in this massive offensive. When some of these agents were apprehended and the disappearance of nuclear materials, samples of deadly viruses etc. was discovered, there was general panic.

A crises meeting of the super powers was summoned by the president of America, where it was decided that there should be general alert and complete unity among nations. This meeting had been closely monitored by king Awobua, who discovered that although the earthlings were still fogged as to the origin of their problems, they were determined to fight back. Prodded by a suggestion from Dr. Kini, one of his academicians, the king had decided to order the suspension of the offensive against the earth. All Mungongoh agents were withdrawn from the earth, while all flying saucer expeditions to earth ceased. King Awobua was waiting for them to become complacent and forget about the threat from outer space, before striking.

On earth, nations had improved upon their collaboration with each other and ceased all aggressive acts. North and South Korea were now operating on the most cordial terms. China had buried the war hatchet with Taiwan, and the Dalai Lama, who was now living in Tibet, visited China often. The Israeli were assisting Palestine through a lot of construction work and equally had embassies in all the Arab countries, while the Arabs were now speaking about Israel on the friendliest terms. Strategic factories for the production of weapons of mass destruction and other arms had now been transformed into giant factories for the production of house hold goods and other harmless but useful items. Even the Soviet Union had jettisoned communism and totalitarianism and the various socialist republics that had existed within the union were now independent democratic countries.

A blissful situation had settled on earth.

1

After having suspended all offensive actions against the earth, king Awobua did not stop observing it closely. He had managed to be patient for fifteen years and had added another ten for good measure. Although he was determined to sacrifice as much time as possible and lure the humans into complete bliss and inattention, he could not help getting annoyed at their lavish lifestyles. On the other hand, the desire to take over the earth kept prodding him painfully in the ribs and his patience was being thoroughly tried. More than twenty five years had passed since the king had banned any action on earth, but he had remained glued to the earth monitor as if he expected a miracle to happen.

On one faithful day, while he was occupied with his favourite pastime of earth watching, a scene which gored his insides came up. A president was being installed in America with lots of pomp and pageantry. The square in front of the Capitol was swarming with flamboyantly dressed politicians and state officials. There were crowds of happy people all over the place, with millions of other happy people all over the world, glued to their TV screens just to watch the event.

King Awobua's right fist crashed on the bald pate of the closest dwarf's head and as the little fellow crumbled in pain the king buzzed for Mobuh.

"Tell me," he said as Mobuh shuffled in. "Are we going to remain nonchalant while those idiots on earth enjoy themselves like this?" The king was pointing at the large screen.

"It was your royal decree that we stop all activities on earth sir." Mobuh reminded him

"Order or no order," retorted the king, "I have reached the end of my tether and cannot take any more of this. I want some action now." The king shoed the dwarf away and continued

"The other week it was the Russians installing some Czar or whatever you call them these days."

"They are known as Presidents, sir. Empires have ceased to exist on earth and most of these monarchies have been transformed into what they call democracies. But as you know, there is very little democracy on earth." offered Mobuh

"Of course, I know that," said the king. "I have watched presidents even of America dictate many things on state policy. Not to talk of those blokes in Africa who are treated like small gods. Well, whatever title this Russian had decided to assume, the bloke looked as regal as ten Mungongoh kings put together. You should have seen all the military gear and display, not to talk of the quality karakul fur cap the old geezer had, perched on his massive skull."

The king rolled his eyes, took a sip of *mukal* and continued. "By the way, why do they spend so much money on useless things like arms? Is it because they have too much or they enjoy fighting?"

Mobuh shrugged and replied.

"They don't have one good king like we have here. The earth is full of sovereign states, bent on interfering with the sovereignty of others. It works from the level of small traditional chiefs to big presidents and kings. That is why these fights range from tribal and intertribal skirmishes to world wars."

"I watch these scenes often," said the king.

Mobuh sighed "Unfortunately for them, most of the chiefs, presidents and kings are always the wrong persons.

2

They are often too weak, too greedy or too aggressive. If you follow honest assessments from Americans, you would realize that they now have a rare pearl in that guy that you watched just now being installed as president of America. It is not easy to find such a leader on earth. They are either struggling to fill their pockets with tax payers' money, or like those presidents in Africa, stay as long as possible in power, or are struggling to ensure that their son or daughter inherits like in Pakistan and India, or simply enjoy terrorizing, torturing and killing their people like one crazy fellow called Pinochet who ruled over Chile at one time."

"Those earthlings need their heads checked," said the king thoughtfully. "If only they had the slightest idea about our own history."

The people of Mungongoh had once lived on Mars alongside other nations. Mungongoh was lucky to have had a level headed king, who was interested in peace and progress whereas the kings of the other domains were aggressive and always lusted for power. This had resulted in an arms race that had eventually gone out of control and every dime in these nations was invested in the production of nuclear weapons. The king of Mungongoh which happened to be one of the smallest kingdoms, had realized that fighting a war with his neighbours would lead to total destruction. He had therefore concentrated on producing spacecrafts that would fly out his people in case of devastation and had put up a defence system that would give them enough time to escape. The war had finally come and all the other kingdoms had perished, and Mars had become inhabitable. All this had happened far off in history but the people of Mungongoh had a wonderful way of preserving historical data.

King Awobua sighed

"I really need to take over the earth before those fools blast it up the way our ancestors did to Mars."

"True sir and those presidents on earth are getting much more than they deserve. Even some of the Presidents of those very poor and highly indebted African countries have access to virtually every comfort and wealth known on earth."

"You can say that again." concurred the king "But apart from these third world presidents who do virtually nothing but live lavish lives, many earthlings unjustly have access to much while most hard working men and women toil virtually throughout the day and throughout the week for pea nuts. You can see that much money is rather dished out to blokes involved in fruitless occupations or pursuits. Imagine brutes that hammer savagely on an opponent with gloved fists in a boxing bout and earn fabulously for such viciousness."

"Yes sir," agreed Mobuh "and those who make rich earnings for reckless driving in motor rallies, not to talk of some who make more money than Croesus just from shrieking on stage or dancing wild jigs."

"I once watched an earth TV show," said the king, "where a bloke was being highly awarded for taking the big risk of dropping for quite a distance from a plane without the use of a parachute, while another lunatic reaped heaps of money for being foolish enough to take the risk of walking over the Niagara falls on a tight rope. Why would a man want to do such dangerous stunts just for others to watch?"

"It is strange, what earthlings would enjoy sir. Maybe it is idleness, or an attempt to transform their useless lives full of boredom into something interesting. That is certainly why they pretend to enjoy themselves at every turn and opportunity. What pleasure they gain from gliding over jagged cliffs or skiing down steep snow covered slopes, I cannot tell. Would you imagine sir, that some earthlings waste days, climbing dangerous mountain slopes when they would have spent their time more profitably?"

Mobuh was one of those chaps who, once they launch into a topic and observe that they are keenly listened to, do not want to stop.

"And then, there is this frivolous sport they call football." He continued "Blokes dressed in expensive jerseys go chasing after a leather ball, and every other earthling seems to enjoy it and pay well for it."

"Football!" said the king smiling. "That is a noble sport. I spend my time here often enjoying it. It is a pity that those dashed Americans are spoiling foot ball and playing something else. Instead of a ball, they use some spherical object. While football was designed to be kicked mostly, they rather run around the football pitch with the ball in their hands and opponents tackle the chap in possession of the ball in a very aggressive manner."

The king was shifting his left foot as if he was preparing to take a shot.

"Then there are these chaps from Cameroon, Ghana and Ivory Coast. You need to see them at work. There is also this young fellow from the land of Tut Ank Amen. Ah yes, wonderful boys I say. I am thinking seriously of introducing that sport here."

"But you can't do that sir!" said Mobuh with consternation. "Mungongoh has always frowned on frivolities. It is just like those earthly public shows with half naked chorus girls kicking their beastly legs in the air."

"Football is not like that," replied the king. "It is a game for real men. Their legs may be foolishly exposed just like those of chorus girls, but it doesn't quite matter. Think of the swimmers who throng pools or lie enjoying the sun along the beaches on earth, all virtually nude apart from scanty swimming trunks."

"If you say so sir," replied Mobuh. "But now that we don't interact with the earthlings, we can't think of bringing a few of them here to show us how to play this game."

"We shall see about that sometime later" declared the king. "Let us forget about football for now."

Mobuh was wondering what would come next. It landed like a bombshell.

"I want to take over the earth now." King Awobua said firmly.

"But sir," Mobuh started to protest, and then perceiving the determination on the king's face, stopped abruptly.

"I want no objection from you. Go and gather all those lazy bums of yours. Tell them that they have been sleeping long enough. I have given them enough time to have come up with the most impeccable strategy to make me king of the Earth. Tell them to act fast or my lions will have an orgy."

"This will need about a year sir," said Mobuh.

"I am giving one hundred days" declared King Awobua. "In one hundred days I should be drinking vodka and eating caviar in the Kremlin, wallowing in rich champagne and cognac in the Élysée palace, carving turkey in the white house, and sampling stuffed duck with old port wine in Buckingham palace. I would even make regular trips to Njinikom in Cameroon where I would sample the delicious corn fufu, vegetables and *kati kati*."

The king's mouth was really watering with the thought

"There is this other delicacy from another place near this Njinikom that I have just mentioned and the delicacy is called *achuh*. The natives use their fingers artfully to shovel loads of the stuff into their mouths. It looks quite tempting to watch them enjoy their meal." king Awobua licked his lips.

"Your knowledge about places and habits on earth is admirable sir," Mobuh said in a placating manner.

"And why not?" replied the king. "Watching the earth is my favourite occupation. Since I will rule over it some day, I should know everything about it. Did you know that in many countries on earth, some jealous fellows start conniving to push presidents and other rulers out of their position when they have enjoyed power less than thirty years? Then there is this place, America where after you have gained concrete management experience over eight years, they instead block you from continuing and rather bring in a fresh horn to come and start from square one."

"It means that this young coloured president that is expected to take America out of the mess in which it is, and fully unite the Blacks and the Whites, shall be compelled to drop only after eight years?"

"Yes, and unfortunately he is not in Africa where he could easily use his lackeys in parliament to change the law and enable him to continue."

"Those earthlings must be crazy," said Mobuh, "and are quite stupid. Why would any man want to change a wise and good king like you? I hear the world is falling apart because all the good old monarchs are being cleared off by half baked revolutionaries. Look at the situation in Afghanistan and in Iran. The people have known no peace, since their monarchs were toppled, as opposed to Saudi Arabia, Jordan, Dubai and Morocco where monarchs are still reigning and there is relative peace."

"The worst one" continued the king "is having a bunch of rascals they call parliamentarians, who have to make the laws for you to follow, although you are the leader. Imagine that they even have to endorse any decision you want to take. I use those lazy fellows in the IRDI simply as a source of

7

inspiration, and that is how it should be. No one challenges my decisions or laws. That is why many weak presidents on earth are forced to rig elections in order to put as many of their supporters as possible into these parliaments, whereas they should have been able to give unchallengeable orders directly."

The king took a large swig of *mukal*. "That is why I will give a last chance for ideas before I take my final decision. Go to the IRDI and see what they will surface with after this long break."

The king was smart enough not to miss some slight hint of hesitation from Mobuh. He glowered a bit "Gather all those crazy punks of yours and make sure that my one hundred days are respected. It is a lot of time you know."

Mobuh, who had not faced the king's wrath for quite a while, had the temerity to propose that some more waiting should be done as he thought it was still a bit early. The king surprised him by his reaction and bellowing like a cuckolded bull landed on him as if he were one of the dwarfs. Mobuh was saved by his massive size and the fact that the king was used to hammering on diminutive dwarfs, not the big brother of Big Show the wrestler.

The king glared at Mobuh and issued strict instructions on the imminent attack. He switched on his monitor to show Mobuh how the greedy fellows on earth were operating like a combination of locusts and caterpillars, devouring everything they came across.

"Go back immediately to those your numb skulls of the IRDI and tell them that I want immediate action. If there is any foot dragging, I will start with you." the king had concluded.

"I will do everything sir. We shall work very hard. Our brains will tick at three hundred miles per hour, and we will certainly give satisfaction. Rest assured sir" Mobuh was effusive in assuring the king.

The king further threatened to throw Mobuh to the lions, if he remained recalcitrant and contrary to his views.

All over the earth lions are linked to Royalty. An Ethiopian Emperor was dubbed Lion of Judah. Most folk tales from Africa and elsewhere consider the lion as the king of the jungle and give it a lot of respect. Other animals on the other hand, receive less dignifying, or even negative titles or descriptions. Thus while the lion is considered as king of the jungle, other animals are considered as loathsome, cunning, vicious, rapacious etc.

In many parts of Africa, the lion is attributed to royalty and power. In some areas, it is even believed that the local king transforms into a lion to go round on reconnaissance trips of the realm.

This royal image and status for the lion equally existed in Mungonoh, far away from the earth. Way back in the era where the people of Mungongoh shared the planet, Mars with other kingdoms, the lion was a pet reserved for royalties and men of very high status. A king could offer a few lions to another monarch, the way Stalin offered cartons of Armenian cognac to Churchill. A king could offer a lion to a well deserving lord for acts of bravery or loyalty. Some of these lions ended up like white elephants because the cost of keeping such pets was high.

The Lions were so valued that they occupied a priority position in Mungongoh. The wise king, who reigned during the period when Mungongoh was compelled by the explosive situation to move to its present site, had considered the importance of the lion to the people of Mungongoh when preparing against any looming catastrophe. A special space craft had been prepared for them and the required care provided. After landing at the present site however, it was discovered that conditions were rougher and feeding voracious lions became a big problem. The beast had finally become available only to the king and nobody else. Even then, the numbers had dropped considerably until the advent of king Awobua who had taken a special liking for the feline pets. The beasts were the only object that could sway the king's attention a bit from earth watching. He also put the lions into another good use as he claimed. In Mungongoh torture and various forms of corporal punishment were not common, and only one form of death penalty existed, introduced by king Awobua, using the condemned persons as food for his lions. Before king Awobua came to the throne, death penalties were meted only to dwarfs and this was in a different form. Now, the lions served as the hang men or the executioners. Being offered to the lions was the worst way to die in Mungongoh. It equally served as the greatest form of entertainment for the king.

The prospect of being offered to the lions was thus not a pleasant one and even the great Mobuh trembled with fear, at the thought of such a possibility.

2

Mobuh came out of king Awobua's inner sanctum sweating and looking terribly shaken, and virtually frothing in the mouth. A mad dog would have learnt something from him about frothing techniques. He had just been through a very rough time and was almost regretting the fact that he was senior minister and the direct contact with the king. He had never imagined that things could come to the level where the king would actually attempt to smite him, but there it was. He was simply fortunate that he had been alone with the king when this disgraceful occurrence took place. He was considered in Mungongoh with much dignity and respect and an attempt by the king to actually inflict such corporal punishment on him would have brought down his mighty image to the level of the down trodden. But then, the dwarfs were present. He was certain he had noticed something like glee on their faces when the king had administered physical violence on him. Although they were considered dumb, the dwarfs could speak and have fun when given the opportunity. This incidence would possibly be much ventilated within their circles, accompanied with lots of ridicule and laughter. The only good thing, Mobuh thought was that they never mixed with regular Mungongoh citizens. The possibility that news about the incidence would cross to Mungongoh citizens was thus very slim.

He was thinking seriously on the new situation as he entered his spacious office and sat down. Maybe it would be better to brainstorm with Itoff and a few top members before taking the issue to the IRDI. But then, Itoff had failed him woefully in previous attempts.

11

The next obvious thing was to bring down his anxiety with a few large gulps of the expensive strong drink he always kept for such incidences. During the period of inactivity on issues concerning the earth, things had been calm and there was never any risk of being confronted with royal anger. He had virtually ruled Mungongoh, as the king had spent most of his time, mulling over the delay in taking over the earth imposed by circumstances beyond their control.

Mobuh took enough time to calm down completely and look dignified. When he thought he had regained full composure, he decided to summon Itoff after all. Two heads work better than one and he needed support to plan the next step. He would go through some earth scenes on the TV console and reserve a few for his encounter with Itoff.

Mobuh took another stiff drink and switched on his earth monitor. A scene in Afghanistan came up where a suicide bomber had just taken down ten relief workers along with him. In another scene in Iraq another suicide bomber had put an end to the sinful lives of fifteen Christians, causing much grief and mourning. 'Serves them right for shunning the great cause of Islam and embracing Christianity' the maniac as he pulled the trigger was going to die along with the infidels. He was rather dreaming of the virgins who would receive him.

As Mobuh continued to watch, a scene in America showed a serious storm that was raging and sweeping down houses along its path. Somewhere in Japan an earthquake was wrecking havoc, accompanied by a horrifying scene of mangled bodies and extensive destruction. It was actually a bloody scene. Out in East Africa, wild animals had gone on the rampage. While lions, cheetahs and leopards were feasting on some villagers, rhinos, and elephants were stampeding through other villages, goring and crushing every living thing in heir path. Farms and village houses were all rendered useless in their wake. In other corners of Africa, civil wars were eminent as incumbent presidents were clinging to power though rejected by the people.

So much was going wrong with the world, and if Mungongoh could push all these disasters to the absolute limit, King Awobua would achieve his life's goal. But then, the earthlings were doing quite much to counter all forms of disaster. Mobuh sighed and switched over to another scene. A cathedral in Asuncion was jammed full with faithful praying to God to rid the world of all calamities. Up in the USA, several crises meetings were holding to check various forms of trouble ranging from terrorists to natural disasters. There were meetings comprised of experts in various fields while other meetings were dominated by politicians.

'The earthlings are leaving no stone unturned to counter crises situations.' Mobuh thought loudly. He buzzed for his secretary and asked her to get Itoff.

"You look very worried sir," she said in a concerned manner.

"I am fine," replied Mobuh. "And don't stand there clucking about whether I look worried or not. Call for Itoff immediately, and brew me some kola coffee."

"Right away sir," the efficient secretary replied and went out.

Mobuh was still concentrated on his earth monitor when Itoff came in.

"You wanted to see me sir?" he asked

"Sit down." ordered Mobuh gruffly, as he continued staring at the monitor.

"I am sure you and our colleagues of the IRDI have had a long rest. Your brains should be fresh, ready to crack the greatest puzzles."

"Is there something the matter sir?" asked Itoff confused

"You remember we have some work that we left uncompleted?"

"May I ask what kind of work sir?" Itoff was still confused

"On earth," replied Mobuh.

"On earth?" Itoff asked.

"You seem to have forgotten that Mungongoh simply suspended activities on earth," said Mobuh. "The king has not cancelled out the idea of taking over the earth."

"Ah that? Yes I now remember sir," said Itoff.

"Good!" said Mobuh. "These jerks on earth are enjoying a bit too much" He pointed a podgy finger at a scene where champagne was flowing and there was a lot of grilled meat and sea food to sample. "They actually seem to be bent on finishing everything before we take over."

"But they have been increasing productivity and production on earth," replied Itoff. "They are creating the fat on which they are feasting."

"That is no reason why they should be walloping all the stuff at that rate." Mobuh insisted. "They should be more sparing in their consumption rate or we may not meet any of the good stuff when we take over. The alarming rate at which these earthlings plunder the see frightens even them. Anyway, the king is fed up with waiting. He now wants action."

"What type of action?" Itoff was alarmed.

"We have to attack the earth and annihilate all these blokes who keep wolfing up all the good stuff at such an alarming rate."

Itoff was quite aware of the fact that the king was eager to put through his plan of conquering the earth, but he had never thought it would be so soon.

"That is a good idea," he said, trying as much as possible not to contradict anything. I should summon a meeting for next week l suppose."

"Tomorrow!" replied Mobuh with emphasis. "I give you only till tomorrow by nine o clock."

As Itoff looked on in surprise, Mobuh continued.

"Everybody has to get back to work now. The king has already given you a long rope to drag. I want serious results now."

"What should we do sir?" Itoff asked.

"Summon a meeting of the IRDI," said Mobuh. "Let us see what next we should do. We need to know how to continue with the mass attack, or maybe your team has other ideas? Let us hear them. As I said earlier, you can put the meeting for tomorrow in the morning."

3

The summons for the meeting was quite brief and sounded quite urgent. Every member of the Institute of Research for the Development of Ideas (IRDI) received the message and clearly understood that no late coming or absenteeism would be tolerated. It was certainly a most important meeting.

"Maybe king Awobua has choked on his *mukal* and died suddenly." Fulumfuchong said in a joke to one of his close friends and colleague when he got to the meeting venue.

All the tough eggs of the IRDI were present and perplexed. One would have expected a lot of changes in the physical appearance of the members of the IRDI, given the extended interval of more than two and a half decades. Given their long lifespan however, not much had changed in their external features After they had all settled down expectantly, Mobuh came in with Itoff and both took their important places reserved for such important men.

Mobuh was resplendent in his *dalla*, a flowing colourful robe with some intricate patterns. It was worn with trousers of the same material and crowned with a beautiful cap with tassels. The design of the *dalla* and the quality of the material determined the status and class of the person wearing it. The best ones were worn by the members of the IRDI, while the king and Mobuh had very special ones made for them by the best designer. As for the ordinary citizens of Mungongoh, their *dallas* were of a cheaper cloth and design. The Mungongoh females dressed in another form of *dalla*, made of the same cloth like the men's. It went with a skirt of the

17

same material or a cloth tied around the loins and allowed to flow freely.

"Everybody is welcome to this meeting". Mobuh said importantly. "I am sure all of you are anxious to know why we have called you here so suddenly and in such a hurry. It is quite simple. Your king is tired of waiting indefinitely for the time when we will take over the earth. I hope you did not all go into slumber during the break. You were rather supposed to continue figuring out how we would clear off the humans from the earth. The king has decided that the period of waiting is over .This meeting is therefore the first of the series that we shall hold in order to develop sound strategies for conquering the earth. The king has every thrust in us and is certain that we will give him satisfaction. Despite the simplicity of the task he has given us up to a hundred days to succeed. Of course, l don't need to tell you what can happen to you if you fail."

Mobuh looked round meaningfully and announced "Let deliberations start".

There was a general murmur in the hall as everybody was appreciating the situation in his or her way.

"The hypocrite" whispered Fulumfuchong to the colleague he had joked with earlier about the king choking on his *mukal*. "The best brains in Mungongoh have spent decades trying to bring up the winning idea and yet no success has been achieved, but here he goes talking about the simplicity of the task."

"Shhhhh!" warned the colleague.

Fulumfuchong was not disturbed. The general hullabaloo would certainly drown off his side whispering.

Mobuh allowed the general disorder for ten minutes, and then decided to put an end to it.

"Silence all of you. I did not summon you hear to come and buzz like a swarm of bees. I want ideas."

Funkuin requested for and was given the floor.

"Before we stopped sending agents down to earth, quite a considerable amount of material had been stolen and brought here. We can take some time, make powerful bombs and knock off those damned earthlings."

"Are you sure of what you are saying?" Itoff asked

"She is right" rumbled an old bloke with a walrus moustache. "Lots of materials had been brought up before the king wisely suspended activities. Given ample time, we can develop enough pestilences to shower on the earth."

Several other ideas came up but none was strong enough to carry the day. Besides, there were always strong counter opinions.

Finally Fulumfuchong who had been silent throughout, jumped up and said. "This is a very delicate issue and we should not rush over it. I suggest we go home and take ten days to think it over before meeting here again."

"The idea is good" said Mobuh, "but ten days is too much. Let's meet back here in five days."

Five days passed very fast and the academicians settled down in their usual hall for the next meeting. Yivissi proposed using gas but the idea was quickly rejected on the premise that there were already very many gas masks on earth and much could be produced within short notice. Another academician proposed fire, but the idea too had great limitations. Food poisoning was proposed by one of the old witches. "They live to eat, so all of them will eat our poisoned food." she had insisted.

"But how do you get poison to the tons of varied food eaten all over the earth every day?" Itoff asked. "The French enjoy frog legs and oysters, while crickets, termites and caterpillars are delicacies in some West African villages. I even noticed that cockroaches are sought for in China or one of those places in the Far East. There are vegetarians in India, Tsampa eaters in Tibet, lovers of Manioc in South America, and those who thrive on breadfruit in Samoa, Tonga and Tahiti."

The next morning the meeting took off in the morning, with Itoff presiding. After Itoff opened the meeting and waited for ideas, he almost got frustrated. That day, nothing concrete came up and the meeting was adjourned to the next day.

"So far" said Itoff, "we don't seem to have surfaced with any super idea that would enable us face the earth with a devastating war. The time that the king gave is running out and we all face his wrath."

"May be we could have better ideas that do not necessitate massive action. I think we should live the floor open for any ideas, even if it is not full scale war," said Yivissi.

"Whatever it is, it must be a full scale attack," said Itoff.

After a brief period of silence, there was some reaction from a middle aged professor of philosophy with a blotched face.

"I think I have a unique approach. We cannot wage a full scale war on the earthlings because of obvious limitations, including man power, fire power and the intricacies of ridding the earth of humans without rendering it inhabitable. Instead of waging a war on the earthlings, I suppose that we push them to do it themselves. We shall make the earthlings fight and destroy each other"

"I think you have a problem there" said a professor of history. "The earthlings have fought many wars, including two world wars, without eliminating even as many humans as

20

our Spanish flue did. Now, they have even put in place, institutions for avoiding destructive wars. How do you suppose to push them into a more destructive global war?"

"The arms race is still on. The fight to dominate the world is still strong among powerful countries. Another global war can still come, depending on its source," the blotch faced professor replied. "The two world wars always started in Europe and concentrated in Europe. Africa and Latin America participated only timidly and were not fully involved. This time we start from Africa and Latin America and drag the world powers of the north to get involved."

"That is a strange idea," said Funkuin.

"Yes, but quite simple. If you are observant, you will see that every totalitarian, reactionary or corrupt regime in Africa or Latin America has a super power in the North behind it. At the same time, each of these countries has revolutionaries lusting for power, operating from Europe or internally as terrorists. We use these hot blooded revolutionaries to destabilize these third world countries in Africa and lure them into a situation of conflict and confusion. This will likely push America, Russia, France etc. into conflict that may result in nuclear war." The professor proposed.

"Your idea is not quite clear to me," said Itoff. "Could you be more explicit?"

"Start with the aspect of destabilizing African countries," said another member of the IRID. "How do you propose to do that?"

"To me, they have already been destabilized," said another member of the IRDI. "The American secrete service agencies have done a lot of havoc out there."

"Let me explain better," said the chap who had launched the idea. "The real root of the problem between America and the Soviet Union has always stemmed from the fact that each party wants to spread its ideology to as many countries of the world as possible, and through this, control the affairs of these countries. When the USSR entered anywhere, America immediately condemned their presence and did everything to uproot them. My idea thus works on the fact that the Russians will fall behind revolutionaries while America will do everything to maintain reactionary bourgeois in power.

"You fail to realize that things have changed a bit on earth. The Soviet Union has collapsed and America is no longer sponsoring the overthrow of governments that they suspect are leaning to the east," Fulumfuchong said.

"I know that," replied the speaker. "But the rivalry has lived on. Each one of these countries still wants to have more influence in world politics. Even countries like France clash with America once in a while for tampering with any of their former colonies, which the French still consider as private property."

"So, what are you really proposing?" asked Itoff.

"The idea is to push such conflicts which for now appear latent, into a violent stage."

"Do you think that can work?" Asked Funkuin.

"I wonder," said Fulumfuchong. "There is a lot more cooperation among African countries these days. You have the OAU waxing strong. Then, you have active regional and sub regional cooperation. Even internal strife has reduced considerably in these countries as most of the volatile revolutionaries are frustrated by support that the corrupt third world presidents get from the superpowers and the determination of the old men to remain in power until their children are ripe enough to take over. Let me assure you that apart from conflicts in some isolated spots, most of the populations have relapsed into a docile acceptance of old undemocratic leaders. In some cases most of the key persons have been bought over and even beg these old inefficient presidents to stay on for eternity. How then do you propose to create problems in these African countries, which will provoke such a situation that can split the big countries over which side to support?"

"That is just what we should exploit," said the professor with the idea. This situation cannot continue forever. While the old top executives are continuously being flattered by those who feast on the crumbs from their tables, true patriots are simmering with anger and boiling point is not far off."

"That is quite true," said a youngish female member of the IRDI. "Things are going out of hand and America and the other big capitalist countries are turning a blind eye because of some foolish belief that a country does not interfere in the sovereignty of others. That is rubbish. Until America, Russia, France, Britain and Germany work together and impose democracy by force in these African countries, the old blokes at the helm will plant themselves deeper into power and create dynasties. The future might become really explosive."

"Thanks Doctor Yivissi." the man whose idea was under scrutiny said to her in gratitude.

"Besides," continued the inspired Dr. Yivissi "the fear of anti Semitism, extremism and Islamic fundamentalism has replaced the fear of the spread of communism. America and the West now support decadent regimes like the one in Syria, which they believe can be used to counter the activities and check the spread of extremist groupings within the volatile region. They have thus turned a blind eye to simmering situations in countries like Egypt, Algeria, Tunisia etc. What we need now is to accelerate the process and enable all the African countries to reach that boiling point together. I assure you the populations of these countries may appear docile for now but serious trouble is brewing."

"And what will happen?" asked Dr Funkuin "The old greedy presidents backed by their savage armies will strike back viciously The inhabitants of these third world countries will simply kill each other and all the other countries of the world will still be there, and these other countries are rather the ones capable of preventing us from taking over the earth."

"That is what you think," replied the former speaker. "However, if you analyze the situation properly, you will see that there will be lots of interest in the situation and the superstars who have nuclear power will be split when it comes to supporting one side or another in each country. This multiple disagreements will certainly lead to an extreme situation, and before you know what is happening, the earth will explode."

"Have you thought of any way to push the great powers to react to the situation the way you assume?" asked Doctor Funkuin

"I have an idea I want to try. The African and Latin American revolutionaries and strong opposition parties do not need too much to strike against the governments. With a little support from us they will be capable of rising. When it starts in one or two countries, the others will be encouraged to rise. Mind you that when we support the opposition, patriots, revolutionaries or what you call them to strike successfully in a country where America has great interest and supports the regime fully, we give the impression that the support has come from Russia or France. When we do the same in a country where Russia has great interest we give the impression that the support has come from America. Since they use mostly conventional weapons in Africa, the struggle will be a bit drawn out, thus giving enough time for the super powers to get angry enough, get in and destroy themselves"

"Does the idea sound convincing enough?" asked Itof, addressing the whole assembly of tough brains

"I have lots of doubts about the whole thing," said Dr Funkuin. "We are supposing many things here whereas we have tried concrete ideas like the Neutron bomb and failed. What can one then expect from a project that depends on human instincts? Those humans are quite smart and need something that does not allow for suppositions."

"I think we should try it," said one ponderous academic. "After all we don't seem to have any other proposals."

"We are supposed to work on concrete proposals not just on any idea just because it has been brought up," said Itoff sternly.

"It is not an empty idea, if you ask me," said Fulumfuchong "although it depends very much on the animal instincts of the humans. The possibility that they may decide to be more human than animal just like in the case of the neutron bomb, is still there. However, I rather think that the possibility of the law of the jungle prevailing this time is greater. Yes, I can safely say that the idea has more than 50% chances of succeeding."

Funkuin gazed at him with much animosity.

"That is still not good enough," said Itoff.

"That is what I was just saying." Funkuin stepped in. "Just look at the case of the neutron bomb where outbreak of war was most certain. The earthlings still managed to behave themselves and maintain peace. I tell you, those dashed earthlings are too scared of war, especially when the immediate outcome is difficult to predict. The earthlings are putting up too many checks and balances, and even all the present day Hitlas and Attilas have too many ropes around their necks."

"We'd better drop it then," said a white haired professor.

"That is agreed," said Itoff, "but what do we take back to Mobuh and the King?"

Brainstorming continued for another three days but nothing concrete was forthcoming. The atmosphere within the IRDI became sombre and gloomy as the possibility of being offered to lions became more and more certain.

An academic who could easily compete with the largest sumo wrestler in terms of size and appetite, finally brought in some life. His idea immediately sounded wonderful to some of the desperate members of the IRDI even before it was well explained.

"Those earthlings believe fervently in a God and while claiming that God is almighty and all powerful they equally attribute lots of powers to Satan. In many cases, they give the impression that Satan rules the earth and God is fighting a lost battle to take it back."

"Where are you driving to?" asked Itoff

"Let's work on this Satan theory. Let us make it a reality." The flabby professor replied.

"You know very well that there are very many atheists on earth and these do not believe in Satan or any supernatural being. Satan is simply evil that has been personified," said Funkuin. "This Satan thing is far-fetched."

"There are lots of things that occur on earth," said the obese IRDI member "that convinces people of all works of life, the religious, non believers, traditionalists and brave men, that there are super natural forces that affect the lives of most earthlings. In many places like Africa, the existence of Satan is grossly mixed up with native belief. That is why in Nigeria, even some Catholic priests believe in the existence of gods, goddesses and spirits in rivers, seas and even streams, all worshipping Satan. Pentecostal churches that abound here, stage manage sessions of *deliverance* as they call it, where evil spirits and demons are supposedly cast out of innocent victims. In Europe where traditional beliefs had been jettisoned long ago, many persons still belief in the existence of Satan and his powers.

"These are common occurrences on earth," said Dr Funkuin. "How do we use these and the devil to destroy the earth?"

"Just what I said," replied the massive professor "Let's make it become a reality."

"Interesting," said Itoff "Tell us how."

"I can see the work of the genius coming up," said Fulumfuchong. "I am really interested."

The flabby professor cleared his throat and started

"The earthlings believe in fake pastors and prophets who claim to have super healing powers. These are charlatans who use Satan to frighten unsuspecting blokes into contributing heavy sums to be *delivered*. These propagators of the devil theory are very smart and attribute the slightest problem any member of their congregation has to the work of the devil and thus create a way of duping innocent people and swindling their hard earned cash through healing. The slightest positive outcome that may occur by chance is hailed far and wide whereas the many failures are blamed on the strength of the devil or the fact that the afflicted person was not praying hard enough. The very few chance successes in these street side churches combined with the multiple problems on earth, have swayed many Christians from a God they believed in but who worked clear miracles only in the days of Jesus. Superstitious earthlings believe more and more that the devil has become very powerful, so powerful that

27

regular priests and pastors have no power over it. They now blindly follow these pastors who claim to have special powers. They claim that God talks to them every day and gives them powers to conquer the devil. They have thus become champions in the act of casting away demons during deliverance sessions, healing, enabling success in life and exams, granting riches, and even making it easy to be accepted by beautiful women."

"You want us to exploit this situation?" Itoff asked.

"Sure," replied the professor. "I have thought over the possibilities for long. Initially I thought we should create a serious strife between religious denominations, groupings and followings. There is much strife between them already but not enough. There is too much tolerance among Christians and some Muslim leaders collaborate closely with Christians. This tolerance is also fuelled by the fact that many earthlings are turning into non believers."

"The explanation is becoming too lengthy," said Itoff.

"I am about to land, sir," replied the professor. "I then thought of another option. If we convince the earthlings to actually believe that there is a Satan and that he is taking over the world, we will have prophets of doom emerging from all quarters. With a bit of clever manipulation we could get them struggling to bring about the end of the world."

"That simple?" asked Fulumfuchong

"It is not as simple as that. I have simply given a brief picture. We could then fit in the details and make the idea very complete."

"This is all hogwash," said Yivissi the prettiest and youngest woman in the IDRI. "It is kind of high sounding and not practical."

"I rather think there is something in it," said Dr Funkuin. "If all the details are worked out well, it may have a chance."

"We want certainties, not possibilities" said Itoff. "An idea that is not certain to succeed is not needed here."

"But we have no other option for now," said Funkuin. "And from every indication, if we work hard on this proposal, it will succeed."

"Maybe," said Fulumfuchong. "But let us hear more about it before accepting or rejecting it."

"We shall get into contact with many of these charlatans on earth." continued the professor presenting. "We will then enable them to do a few convincing things that look like miracles. We will for example use apparitions and lots of deceitful things. We could equally send a few agents out there who would act mad or show signs of strange incurable ailments and let these fake pastors cure them. That will enable them to acquire a massive following. With each local charlatan prophet or pastor having a large following, many earthlings will be under our control."

"And what do you suppose to do with this control?" asked Yivissi.

"It may not be clear to you yet, but let me assure you that the next step will be catastrophic for the earthlings. Once all the half wits on earth believe completely in our fake prophets, our next step will be to get these pastors or prophets to lure them into believing that they should prove to their God that they actually believe in him."

The inspired professor looked round for any questions. None came. Everybody seemed to be listening attentively.

"These mad fellows will ask their followers to take poison, cyanide for example. Others will lure their followers into other forms of massive death and these would include drowning thousands in lakes, seas and rivers, gathering in rooms and setting fire to them, falling from cliffs, rolling down from high hills, you name it."

"That is wonderful," said an excited Dr Funkuin. "We could get them to crash in planes, sink their own ships full of passengers and all that"

"But do you think it is that easy to convince an earthling to accept to prematurely take his or her own life using such crude methods as you have explained?" asked Yivissi.

"It is all a matter of timing and convincing." Answered the overweight professor. "After our charlatans 'perform' miracles and convince people that they are actually the true apostles of God, it will not be a big problem for them to convince the people that taking cyanide and surviving was the best way to show God that you really trust him and believe in him. The earthlings will easily fall for that. Why, other charlatans make thousands earthlings of to slave for them while they ride in Rolls-Royces and fly their own private jets. The earthlings will easily take the bait."

"But who are we actually targeting on earth to use for these suicide missions?"

"That is not difficult. The established churches have their standard beliefs and are struggling to keep their followers who keep swaying towards all the new churches that surface every day. While the old established churches mostly have their regular services, prayers and activities, the new churches claim to perform miracles. These miracles keep attracting others, including superstitious atheist. If we assist them in faking these miracles, soon the Catholic, Presbyterian and Baptist populations would all have crossed to these charlatans."

"And once they cross over," said Funkuin. "They would become like putty in the hands of these charlatans, and places them completely at our disposal."

"Your idea now sounds workable to me," said Yivissi "but on earth, there are too many sceptics."

"Maybe, but more of them are naive and very superstitious, especially when it concerns God, Satan and evil spirits," replied the professor.

"Okay," said Itoff. "I still have some doubts about this idea but I have to present something to Mobuh immediately, and there is no better alternative."

"It is watertight!" insisted the professor who had proposed it "The king will be elated and it will work like magic."

4

Itoff took off for Mobuh's office where the idea was presented in detail. Mobuh thought it was okay and immediately shoved off to the king's private abode. But then, he was still not certain as to how the king would take it so he went into the king's presence with a lot of apprehension. He was fully aware of the fact that the king and actually reached the end of his tether and had become very nervous and unpredictable

"Let's hear what you have this time," the king said, immediately he stepped in.

Mobuh was surprised to see Ngess standing respectfully by the corner where attending dwarfs waited.

Ngess had been summoned by the king himself in anticipation of Mobuh's arrival with the latest idea developed by the members of the IDRI. He had rushed to respond to the king's call immediately and had been made to stand in a corner and wait just like one of the dwarfs. The inconsiderate king would not offer him even his foot stool to sit on.

"Greetings to the great and mighty one," said Mobuh in the most flattering manner. "I have brought the latest idea from the IRDI and this time….."

"Cut it off" roared the king. "What good thing can come from that house full of decadent fools? I wonder how they came to have the 'Professor' title that they all bear."

Mobuh waited patiently till the king had run out of steam.

"I am surprised to see Ngess here sir," said Mobuh.

"I need your ideas vetted before I rely on them," replied the king. "From now on any idea from you blokes will be examined by this lowly man before we pass it. I have wasted a lot of money and time on the foolish ideas you previously served me."

'The hypocrite' thought Ngess. 'He Knows, I can have the intelligence to crosscheck ideas from the greatest professors of the land, yet he treats me like a dwarf.'

"Can I go ahead then with the new idea?" Mobuh asked

"Go on!" said the king impatiently. "I hope you are listening attentively, Ngess."

"Yes sir," Ngess replied.

Mobuh presented the idea in vivid detail including the questions and arguments presented and the explanations that followed. Ngess was quiet throughout listening attentively. He was aware of the fact that the king was unpredictable and inclined to sudden violent reactions.

At the end of Mobuh's presentation, king Awobua turned to Ngess

"What do you think?" he asked. It did not occur to him that Ngess would need time.

Ngess was quite smart however, with a brain ticking like a clock. He had barely had time to come up with an appropriate answer which he knew must be given o the king at once. He therefore spoke the first sensible thing that came to his mind, just to gain time.

"Theoretically, the idea sounds good, but practically. I have lots of doubts," he said.

"That is not very explicit," said the king.

Ngess adjusted his body on his tired legs. "Before we pass the idea, let's make an inventory of the demented pastors we would use. It is good to know how many demented pastors we can hook on in a hurry. This kind of move has to be sudden and massive. If that can be guaranteed and full action all over the earth, then we could develop a little push from this side and achieve what we want."

34

The king turned to Mobuh. "The idea had not been dismissed completely by Ngess, so we will still consider it," His tone was therefore moderate

Mobuh heaved a sigh of relief. There was a window of hope left open and if well exploited could deliver.

"Go back to the IRDI and follow the recommendations of Ngess. He is quite right," the king said finally.

Mobuh went out with Ngess to his office. There, he sat down, took a few stiff drinks without bothering to offer any to the lowly Ngess, belched loudly and said

"Now, tell me the truth. Do you think this idea will work?"

"It all depends," replied Ngess guardedly. He had had some time now to consider the whole idea and the more he thought, the less convinced he became about it.

"Depends on what?" asked the beleaguered Mobuh.

"It depends on whether you will find any men of God on earth, mad enough to destroy themselves and their following."

"Why do you say that?" asked Mobuh

"Most of these men of God on earth are rather men of the world. They enjoy beautiful women, good food and wine, luxury cars, beautiful comfortable homes, and they always dress to kill. I am sure they equally wear the exquisite FM perfumes and are the best customers for the market for jewellery and gold objects."

"That sounds normal," said Mobuh.

"It may," replied Ngess. "but it also means that these men of God have access to all these good things, thanks to the contributions made by their following."

"True," said Mobuh, understanding at last. "And when we encourage people to go to them, the result will be that their church collections will increase wonderfully."

"Sure!" concurred Ngess "and therefore, even the most demented ones will hesitate to take away their luxurious lives or the lives of those who provide the luxury."

"That sounds like it," said Mobuh. "What do you suggest we do now?"

"The king is waiting for a reply and we cannot let him down without trying" suggested Ngess. "The IRDI is made up of the top brains of the realm. One of them could surface with a sound idea that could make this theory actually work. Besides, we need to try first and see whether we could trace any men of God worth using." Ngess was aware of the fact that no matter how much the members of the IRDI wracked their brains, nothing concrete would come out of them, but he wanted to remove the burden from his own shoulders.

When Mobuh went back to the IRDI, he presented Ngess's suggestions as if he had thought of them himself. He lied to the members of the IRDI that he had not been to king Awobua yet, because he had doubts that needed to be straightened out first. After much thinking, he had decided to come back so that together, they could carry out a thorough search and actually identify concrete pastors to use. Mobuh was known to be the greatest man in the kingdom, after the king of course, but was not actually considered as sharp, but the members of the IRDI all accepted that he had done some good thinking.

"Yes, I propose that we scan the earth for candidates" said Mobuh.

"The earth is not only full of greedy and fake men of God, but also of eccentric and demented persons. We shall easily find many of them to use."

The largest screen in the hall was switched on and the search started. It moved round the world, automatically picking out possible candidates. Further screening of the candidates picked up was necessary to ensure that they would actually go to the extent of dragging their following and themselves into horrifying death. The screening had to be thorough so as not to identify fellows who could develop cold feet and back out at the last moment. Virtually all the hopeful cases were eventually eliminated and after several gruelling hours, they had only picked out a fellow called Jim Jones. Further search the next day landed on another lunatic somewhere in Uganda. The search continued for three days with thousands of possible candidates identified but rejected after close scrutiny. Finally the idea had to be given up.

Mobuh was faced with the task of going back to the king with the disappointing news but before that, he summoned Ngess to his office.

"Ngess," he said, "you were in the king's presence when I went in to present this idea of using fake pastors."

"Yes sir."

"Has the king called for you again?"

"No sir, not yet sir," Ngess replied.

"You think he will call for you?" Mobuh asked.

"I can't say sir," replied Mobuh. "but I am ready to go to him anytime he calls."

"Now that the idea cannot work, what will you tell him?" asked Mobuh

"He has not called for me sir," replied Ngess.

"If he did?" insisted Mobuh "What reason would you give for the fact that the idea will not work? Remember that the earth is supposed to be full of demented persons that could easily have been lured into the plan."

"Yes sir," replied Ngess. "The problem is that most of these mad men who pass for men of God do not even believe that God exists. On the other hand all of them prefer to stay alive and enjoy themselves thoroughly."

When Mobuh went back to the king later, he found him watching some earth scenes keenly. It would appear, after identifying Jim Jones as a possible suicidal pastor, the IRDI had inadvertently prompted him into action. Gathering his flock somewhere around Guyana, he persuaded all of them to take cyanide to show the extent of their faith. Faith in God alone he claimed would save all of them from the deadly effects of the poisonous substance. On the other hand, refusal to take the poison would mean choosing Satan in place of God. King Awobua was watching the lifeless bodies of men, women and children strewn all over the place.

"This idea really works. I hope you can rope in a few thousands of such fellows. We would actually turn the world upside down." He said as Mobuh waddled in. "And do you know?"

Mobuh waited in respectful silence for the king to continue.

"This is the best way for these earthlings to be cleared off from the earth. Yes, no destructive bombs and no virulent diseases in the atmosphere, although the stench from decaying human bodies may affect the air around for a while."

"It looks quite effective sir," said Mobuh, glancing at the screen. He winced at the thought of bringing out the disappointing information he had to transmit. He rallied courage and continued

"We are sorry sir, but after a very thorough search, only this Jim Jones and a handful of others were found to be capable of assisting in our plan."

"What?" exclaimed the king.

"We are really sorry sir but many of such prophets on earth actually want to live long and live well and don't actually have real faith in God the way they are supposed to have.

Many of them do not honestly believe in heaven and an afterlife."

"I thought you painted them as maniacs and lunatics." the king said.

"Some are quite demented, but even then, you would agree with me that very few mad men on earth are prepared to commit suicide."

"What a pity that most of the earthlings are not mad enough." The king sighed. "You guys should act fast. My deadline still holds and this time nobody will be spared, even you."

Mobuh left the king's abode determined to push the fellows in the IRDI hard and employ every possible method to give the king satisfaction. After all, being a chief minister on earth would be quite a great thing. He imagined how those prime ministers in some of those small impoverished countries on earth lived lavishly and expensively. How would it be then to be chief minister in a government that covered the whole earth?

5

Mobuh's instructions to Itoff later on in his office were quite severe. The frown on his face, his gestures and even the simple sound of his voice were quite hard, meant to intimidate and push Itoff to do even the impossible. There was no wavering and Itoff understood that they were all getting to a point where their otherwise comfortable lives were seriously threatened. Itoff eventually left to summon his IRDI mates, equally bent on achieving results.

After two days of thinking, proposing, discussing and rejecting, they had gone nowhere. On the third day there was again another hand up with yet another idea.

"I have been looking at this thing closely for a while and I have noticed certain trends on earth," said a professor of meteorology. "May be we don't need to do anything. We could sit down and wait for them to destroy themselves."

"That is not quite clear said Itoff. Earthlings enjoy life and want to live for as long as possible. Even those who attempt suicide end up feeling very lucky if they are saved or their suicide attempts fail. How do you think they would want to destroy themselves if not provoked to the extreme?"

"I was thinking more of the way they abuse the environment," said the professor. "Most of them may not have suicidal tendencies but their foolishness and recklessness could equally lead them to wiping out mankind. You see, many earthlings believe that their God actually gave them a balanced world. There is enough land on which land animals and man live and exploit for food and other sources of livelihood. There is enough water for sea animals to proliferate and even provide a steady source of nourishment to man and many animals. There is air to breathe in the atmosphere and an established way of recycling it through plants. There are natural ways of reproduction and timely plagues and diseases to check an over increase in population."

"Are we going back to school?" complained another professor.

"Give him time." growled Itoff. "Let him say what he wants. Maybe we would arrive somewhere."

"Thank you sir." The speaker who had the floor said gratefully to Itoff. "Among animals, there are herbivores that live on grass and plants and carnivores that feed on them. But you see, while accepting that all these natural gifts, checks and balances were put there by their God, these same humans have been constantly abusing the environment without the least thought about tomorrow. Bush fires have become very common in third world countries where subsistence farming is rife and traditional methods of rearing cattle is common, resulting in much of the vegetation that provided some balance, being replaced. In developed countries, heavy industrial plants spew obnoxious smoke into the air and produce lots of toxic waste. After killing all the fish in their rivers through the careless disposal of toxic waste from industrial plants, much of this waste is now smuggled into developing countries where corrupt senior officials fill their pockets and provide protection and cover."

"We could clap for this thorough lecture on the earth and its habits but where does it lead us?" asked Dr. Funkuin.

"Many destructive things," replied the meteorology expert. "The ice in the poles which constitute the best form of preserving excess water is melting at a terrible rate. The weather is thus disrupted in many parts of the world and destruction from floods and storms is increasing at an alarming rate."

"True," said Yivissi." I have watched many such scenes on earth."

The meteorologist smiled appreciatively.

"The air is becoming terribly polluted through wastes from industrial processes, bush fires, and lots of other causes. Sulphur dioxide and other substances detrimental to the ozone layer remain a constant threat. With the ozone layer depleted, destructive rays from the sun will easily penetrate down to the earth and cause much havoc. I tell you, it is just a matter if time before the earthlings are wiped out."

"Do you know how long we have to wait for this to take place?" asked Fulumfuchong.

"Not really" admitted the professor. "It will have to take some time though, but not too long."

"Let me show you something then," said Fulumfuchong, switching on the large monitor for all to see. The scene was an international conference on climate change. Countries were blaming one another for being the main cause and propagator of the problem, but all accepting that it was a serious problem that had to be tackled carefully and immediately.

"What you see here," said Fulumfuchong, "is proof that the earthlings have become aware of their destructive lifestyle and are prepared to work for the preservation of the environment."

The meteorologist jumped up.

"That may be so but this awareness is coming too late. Destruction has gone too far and I wonder whether mere international conferences can bring back the balance in the ecosystem to what their God is supposed to have created. Even then, adjusting to proper behaviour is not easy. You see how difficult it has been to convince the Japanese to give up shark fins as a delicacy or to refrain from hunting whales. In the third world, bush meat is not only the principal source of meat to some, but is equally considered a delicacy to all. I tell you, it will be very difficult to turn them round."

"I agree with you," replied Fulumfuchong. "But the fact that the earthlings are doing something about it shows that their eventual destruction from this environmental threat shall be considerably delayed or even cancelled out completely. Climate change wiped out dinosaurs on earth but other species kept on thriving. Many animal species have disappeared but man keeps ensuring a long life for himself. You have observed before that earthlings are very smart and can walk out of seemingly impossible situations."

"Apart from that," said Itoff, this idea of a possible catastrophe through climate change rather means that we should act fast and destroy the earthling so that we take over an earth worth living in. If we allow the earthlings to stay on and continue abusing the environment, floods and other natural hazards from this abuse may render the earth completely inhabitable, even for us. You see, it is not only nuclear power that can lay waste to an area."

"Professor Itoff has brought out the real point," said Funkum, giving the impression that previous arguments presented by Fulumfuchong were far off the mark. "I suppose that means we close this ridiculous idea and continue."

"That is it," said Itoff decisively. "Besides, we cannot keep waiting for something whose outcome we cannot quite determine. Don't forget that the king wants immediate action not some future possibility without any concrete basis. This idea is rejected."

In his office, Mobuh was thinking deeply. The king had relied on him almost completely on matters concerning Mungongoh. With a king constantly away in his palace, he was virtually the first citizen in Mungongoh. His wife enjoyed her elevated position in society to no extent. She loved being bowed to and revered by all of Mungongoh. But now, things were almost going out of hand. The big brains in the IRDI were not surfacing with any winning idea that would give the king satisfaction. Were it not that Itoff was his brother in-law, he would have pushed the king to offer him to the lions. May be that would cool the king down a bit. The king was quite unpredictable now as things kept dragging on and could easily turn on him.

Mobuh shuddered as he switched on his earth monitor and watched a few earth scenes. He landed on some United Nations Security Council sessions. America and Russia were disagreeing over many issues but the delegates socialized well after the sessions and went drinking champagne together in very relaxed moods. Even on situations where the Iranian Ambassador took the rostrum and blasted America and its allies to no end, where one would expect serious tension and possible conflict, the Americans simply boycotted and waited for their turn to talk back. Things were too peaceful on earth. No sign of war. He switched over to another scene and quickly switched it off because he came across some football fans celebrating victory in grand style. What he needed was misery on earth just the way the earthlings were making his life and the king's, miserable.

He switched to another earth scene. It was somewhere in Tanzania where man eating lions were prowling around ignoring all the game in the bush and looking for human prey. This gladdened him a bit. He continued watching and realized that the wild beasts had reasons for their preference to humans. Despite their high intellect as compared to animals, humans are easier to catch. They can't run, they can't climb trees and cannot even fight back. Mobuh wished he could transform all the flesh eating animals on earth into men eating beasts. Bears, lions and all the wild cats would be looking out for humans to feast on. Even birds of prey like condors, eagles and falcons will together consume thousands of humans each day.

Then the reality struck him. These animals might have access to rural areas but access into developed cities will be difficult. Besides, the humans had guns and other modern artillery with which they could easily wipe out the aggressive animals. Besides, animal population has considerably been reduced by human activities.

Mobuh decided to call for Ngess.

When Ngess arrived thirty minutes later Mobuh was already working on some state matters.

"Sit down," Mobuh said to Ngess and continued to concentrate on his work for a while.

Ngess accepted his position of lowly subordinate and did not complain. Finally Mobuh rounded up whatever he was doing and turned to Ngess.

"Ngess," he said.

"Yes sir," Ngess replied.

"Things seem to be going out of hand. My professors do not seem to be coming any closer to developing an idea that would satisfy the king," Mobuh said.

"I am sorry to hear that sir," replied Ngess.

"Do you have any idea that we may present to the king?" Mobuh asked.

"I am not a member of the IRDI sir." Ngess said.

"But the king seems to have confidence in you," said Mobuh.

Ngess was quiet for a while but his mind was working hard. He was neither a professor nor of high standing. The IRDI may propose ideas to the king that end up not bearing fruits, but it was a whole institution on which the king will still have to rely for the next idea. On the other hand, a simple man like him was easily dispensable. One unsuccessful idea from him to the king could result in his being transformed into a meal for the lions. He was aware of the king's anger and the fact that Mobuh would do nothing to defend him the way he defended Itoff and members of the IRDI. It was therefore prudent he concluded, not to give the impression that he was capable of developing any sound idea.

"You see," he reminded Mobuh "developing an idea requires tough brains. The members of the IRDI are all experts in different domains and together can bring out the best idea. Simple men like us can only analyze these ideas that have already been developed by them and bring out loopholes, just like you told the king before. At the level of conception we are lost."

"You are saying you can't help me?" asked Mobuh. "Anyway, what you are saying is true, but since you have the capacity to analyze and bring out weak points, you take how long you need, one week, one month or one year, but I want results at the end. Get back to me as soon as an idea surfaces."

Mobuh buzzed for his secretary.

"Get Itoff for me immediately," he said. At these turbulent times, nobody wanted to take the risk of giving offense to hierarchy, so Itoff dropped everything and hurried to Mobuh's office. Itoff had been having Kola coffee in his office when the call came from Mobuh's secretary. Mobuh could have called him directly but wanted things official so as to impress upon Itoff that his was a serious call.

"No hope yet from your angle?" Mobuh asked as Itoff came in.

"The members of the IRDI are working very hard sir," replied Itoff.

"This type of hard work that is not bearing any fruits," said Mobuh. "I want to remind you that the king's anger will be difficult to contain soon, except something is done. Have any sharp ideas come up?"

"A few sir, but we went to be quite sure. We don't want any failures," said Itoff.

"It had better be," replied Mobuh.

6

The subsequent meetings of the IRDI were hot but not inspiring. Many ideas were proposed but none of them even measured up to the previous ones. The brains of the members seemed to have become empty, if not tired. To guarantee success, Mobuh made it a point of attending all their meetings. This constant presence, meant to bolster the thinking capacities of the professors, did not seem to be helping in any way.

It was Fulumfuchong who finally surfaced with an unexpected idea. When he asked for the floor, it was quickly given to him but with mixed feelings. While assuming that he was certainly coming up with an idea similar to the useless ones that had been rejected, there was still some glimmer of hope that this time, it might be a winner.

"Instead of making war," Fulumfuchong said, "let us make peace."

"What?" everybody said in surprise.

"Let's look at it this way," replied Fulumfuchong. "To wage a war or offensive of any type, we must muster enough force to sack the earth at lightning speed. From past experience, the earthlings have proven that they have the capacity to resist and quickly develop a counter measure to all our attempts at flattening them". If we give them the slightest breathing space, Mungongoh stands the risk of an unexpected riposte from the earthlings, which might end in disaster for Mungongoh."

There was a murmur of shock all around.

"May the king forgive you for having such thoughts, let alone saying them out loud." Mobuh finally managed to say.

"I mean it" continued Fulumfuchong apparently unperturbed. "We could rather go into a relationship with the earth and carry out trade. That will be far better than going in for an expensive offensive with an uncertain outcome. Mungongoh history gives a clear example of how it is better to make peace, not war. All of you here are aware of the fact that if we did not have a reasonable and peaceful king during the period of the big bang in Mars, we would have perished along with the other kingdoms that were ruled by rapacious monarchs."

"You seem to be giving the impression that we are all wasting our time here. You are forgetting the fact that we have been commissioned by the king to look for the best way of taking over the earth without destroying it, so that Mungongoh citizens transfer there. Are you aware of the fact that what you are saying is treason?

"We have virtually exhausted all our strategies that could kill all humans without laying waste the earth. We have used epidemics and monstrous ideas that have all failed. It is equally quite clear that it is not possible to provoke a large scale conventional war, a war that would not involve the use of weapons of mass destruction. If only we could provoke a lasting worldwide conflict, limited to the type of weapons used in the days of Chaka the Zulu, but fought with the violence that could only be witnessed in their hell, then we would succeed in wiping out the earthlings, while everything else remains intact. As you see however, such a war at a global scale is not possible. On the other hand, the earthlings have enough nuclear power to fight back and destroy us if they only knew where we are."

Fulumfuchong was sure that he had convinced most of the members of the IRD as to the futility of continuing with the attempt to conquer the earth, but he was disappointed.

"They don't know where we are and their fire power cannot come anywhere close to us," said Funkuin.

"Maybe," said Fulumfuchong, "but you can never tell what these earthlings can come up with. Don't forget that they have crude observatories that they keep improving upon every day."

"Are you suggesting that one day they will be able to observe us the way we observe them?" asked Yivissi.

"Why not?" answered Fulumfuchong.

"Even if that could happen," said Funkuin, "it would be a long way from now. By then we would already be the occupants of the earth."

"How do you hope to achieve this?" asked Fulumfuchong.

"What was the IRDI created for?" asked Fumkuim aggressively "We are working on it and will soon have a concrete idea on how to take over the earth."

"You think so?" asked Fulumfuchong "I like your optimism. We have been working on this issue for ages and are still far off from the mark. Only on a few occasions did we come even close to anything and that was when my AIDS idea was applied."

"You could keep blowing your own trumpet," said Funkuin, "but it is common knowledge what a terrible failure your idea was. You were not even sure of what you had created and could not give it a name. To prove that the idea was hopeless, the earthlings chose a very ridiculous name for it. A name like AIDS is not worth wagging your tail about."

Mobuh who had been actually boiling throughout these exchanges now stepped in. His face was red with rage. Fulumfuchong had pushed him to boiling point.

"Will you shut up and keep quiet?" thundered Mobuh.

"The king has not given us a choice. He has asked us to look for strategies of crushing the earthlings, not hobnobbing with them. I don't want to hear any more rubbish about collaboration. If you don't have any sound ideas, then listen to the others."

Fulumfuchong subsided into silence but remained thoughtful. What ever was going on again meant nothing to him. When the meeting ended, again without any concrete ideas reached, Fulumfuchong rushed to his office and locked the door. The king had given Mobuh a deadline for the development of a really devastating idea and was prepared to take matters into his own hands and make rash decisions if he did not get satisfaction. Fulumfuchong thus realised that he had a very short time to act to save Mungongoh and the earth. After serious thinking, ideas started coming up. He would link up with a few agents who had been going to earth frequently. Although the king had banned trips to the earth, a few research missions continued, but these made sure that there was no contact with earthlings. He would program a research flight. Then, what next? He finally fell asleep on his table.

7

Fulumfuchong was sitting on the king's chair placed on a pedestal in front of one of the huge cages containing king Awobua's lions. His *dalla* was more magnificent than any that Awobua had ever worn, and he was wearing Awobua's special cap that served as a crown. He had always admired Awobua's magnificent sceptre made of ebony and ivory, an item that was brought in from Mars, and he was grasping this invaluable treasure in his right hand. Just then, he perceived Awobua being brought out in chains from a store in which they kept food for the lions and often kept prisoners condemned to death. He was looking very sad and tired, a remarkable difference from the fiery proud king he knew. Apart from a dirty torn singlet and smudged underpants, he was wearing nothing else. Mobuh and Itoff were also being shoved out of the store by eager hands. Mobuh had folds all over and presented a sight worth seeing. Deprived of his clothes, he looked like a hippopotamus walking upright. He seemed to have rolls of fat everywhere, starting from his toes to his fingertips, not to mention his stomach and jowls. His wife's culinary expertise was actually displayed here.

The trio was led to stand in front of king Fulumfuchong who was expected to either grant pardon or condemn them to be eaten by the lions. He smiled at them benignly as if he was going to order their release, then turned suddenly to the chief executioner and commanded him to throw them, one into each cage. Mobuh and Itoff started screaming out his name, begging for clemency.

Fulumfuchong got up with a jolt and realized that he had had been dreaming. Mobuh and Itoff were pounding on his door and shouting his name as if judgment day was around the corner. Fulumfuchong strode to the door and unlocked it. What he saw was quite different from what he had just been dreaming. A commanding and well dressed Mobuh was standing there, looking so much as if he owned the whole Mungongoh. A pompous Itoff was standing by his side, looking at Fulumfuchong with a lot of disgust.

"The king orders your presence immediately," said Mobuh commandingly. "And what have you been doing behind locked doors, and with your phone off too?"

"I simply fell into slumber sir. I wanted to rest a bit after the heated meeting and since I had some urgent work to do, I saw no need to go home." Fulumfuchong rushed to explain.

So the king's lackeys had rushed to their master to inform him about his suggestion of peace and trade. Fulumfuchong felt sudden fear gush through him. He meekly came out of his office and followed the king's top lieutenants to the king's private abode.

King Awobua was looking glorious in his kingly *dalla*, crowned with a cap of the same cloth as the *dalla*, but adorned with cowries, and huge ebony bangles on both wrists. He did not look like a king who could be overthrown. Neither did he look like a man who would stoop to the level of being offered to lions and be reduced to the lowly position of begging for clemency from another person. Fulumfuchong's fear rose to the limit when the king swerved towards him in his royal chair and eyed him with as much disdain as can be measured.

'He who is down fears no fall' concluded Fulumfuchong as he bowed to the king.

"You are the punk who believes that I am stupid?" roared the king.

"I never said that sir," replied Fulumfuchong, watching out for the king's fists and measuring every statement as if he were measuring medical components in microscopic quantities.

"I was definitely told that you think that my idea of conquering the earth is stupid." the king thundered back.

"Somebody has not been telling you the truth sir" Fulumfuchong dared. "I neither thought nor gave any impression that your idea of conquering the earth is thoughtless. I simply proposed another option which you could consider."

"Are you aware of the fact that I asked for sound strategies of conquering the earth and not for stupid options?" The king was looking as if he could pounce on him with thundering fists.

Fulumfuchong edged back carefully a little and kept watching out for flying royal fists.

"I was simply looking for a way of avoiding casualty sir." Fulumfuchong replied carefully.

"You now seem to be insinuating that my idea of conquering the earth is reckless?" the king growled.

"I am not against your idea sir. In fact all of us here want to see you as the king of the earth. My biggest wish too is to live on earth where there would be plenty. To hell with the earthlings! I am simply afraid of the fact that there may be some problems in the process of executing the idea sir."

Fulumfuchong's face was trickling with sweat. He was perspiring profusely despite the well adjusted air conditioning, as he realized that his fate depended on this brief encounter with the king. His dream seemed to be coming to reality, only this time, he was the one whose life was dangling between clemency and being put at the disposal of the champing jaws of lions.

"I am sorry sir, if my ideas were misunderstood. I was simply cautioning my colleagues to tread carefully so as not to surface with an idea full of dangers."

"What dangers are you talking about?" This time the king asked calmly.

"The earthlings are capable of striking back and that could be disastrous. Even your royal life could be threatened."

This last bit flattered the king some, and to Fulumfuchong's great relief there was a royal reprieve.

"I will spare you this once. But anymore rash ideas shall not be condoned. I want to be king of the whole earth and have no intension of negotiating with anybody. Now take off before I change my mind. Join the others in looking for concrete strategies of taking over the earth. I will personally make sure that all your ideas are closely examined."

Fulumfuchong left the king's chambers with much relief. On the other hand Mobuh and Itoff were quite disappointed. For Fulumfuchong to be let off the hook so lightly was not what they had expected. He went back to his office and sat down heavily on his comfortable chair. His idea was to black out and relax completely. Instead, ideas kept flicking through his worried brain. The demented king had become very dangerous and should go. But then, he was surrounded by stooges like Mobuh and Itoff who would give their last tooth to protect him.

The next morning Fulumfuchong got up from sleep, still convinced that the king should be thrown out. His refreshed mind now started ticking and soon hit on a possible idea. He would request the assistance of some of those earthling presidents. That was the best thing to do. Sell them a few Mungongoh secrets and get their full cooperation. But could he sneak off to the earth without quickening the suspicious minds of Mobuh and Itoff? The two blokes seemed to have appointed themselves guardian angels of the king and were bent on achieving the impossible to make him the king of the earth.

For two days Fulumfuchong was racking his brains as if he were participating in one of those puzzle games for smart brains. During subsequent meetings of the IRDI, he was always physically present but his mind was always far off somewhere. Mobuh finally noticed his aloofness to all deliberations and commented.

"Fulumfuchong, your level of participation has virtually dropped to zero. Don't forget that the king insists that we consider your ideas seriously, but we have received non since then."

"I am sorry," Fulumfuchong replied guiltily. "My mind has been under serious pressure as the days go by and I cannot surface with any good idea to enable our king rule the earth."

"You would not help the king in any way by such a defeatist tendency. Perk up and think. Although we were given a very short deadline by the king, we still have a bit of time. Let's have something from you soon."

Mobuh had inadvertently given Fulumfuchong the key to his problem. It had been there all this while and his tortured brains kept circumventing it. How simple. All he had to do was propose to be sent to the earth with a few selected spies. He would claim that to best attack the earth they needed to spy a bit and uncover loopholes. While on the earth he would rather carry out his plans. One possibility was that he could hand pick agents that he would easily convince and get them over to his side.

Fulumfuchong was humming merrily as he sat having lunch which his servant had just placed on the table. He switched on the TV screen embedded in the wall and selected. Mungongoh had only one station which apart from praising the king, gave very little else. However in the homes and offices of the members of the IRDI, they had the option of watching earth news. They could tune to any station on the earth and watch. Fulumfuchong switched from a scene in Ulan Bator where some Mongols were tending horses in the fields to another one in Kazakhstan where some old Kazakhs were savouring Kumis, fermented mares' milk with a touch of alcohol. The next scene was somewhere in the Kalahari, where some little bushmen were sharing meat just brought in from the hunt. They were all common place scenes, no violence, no anguish and no sorrow. What a peaceful world!

Fulumfuchong searched on and stopped as he came across Somali pirates raiding a cargo ship. The next scene was a drug war in Mexico. Guns, violence, cursing and obscenities galore. 'That is more like the earth.' he thought. 'These are things that Mungongoh could rather join hands with the earth and eradicate for the good of all.'

He dropped the remote control and concentrated on his meal.

8

The next day Fulumfuchong was quite calm during the meeting in the IRDI. A few ideas were tabled, but all lacked weight. Finally Mobuh turned to Fulumfuchong.

"I hope you remember that we are counting on you to wrack your brains hard and come up with something worth relying on."

Fulumfuchong stood up. He wanted to make it look as if he really cared and wanted the satisfaction of the king.

"We have actually been working on this for several weeks, time is actually running out, and we are all very enthusiastic to satisfy our king through the great Mobuh. If we don't come out with something soon, it might become too late."

"We all know that very well," said Funkuin sharply. "What Mr. Mobuh wants is a winning idea, not a reminder as to our predicament."

"She is right," said Mobuh. "Give me ideas."

"Since we have virtually come to the end of our capacity without coming out with a sound strategy," said Fulumfuchong hurriedly, I would think that the solution can only come from the earth."

"You will not stop surprising us." commented Itoff.

"Why the earth?" asked Mobuh. "How do you think the earthlings can give us a solution to their own destruction? You can't be serious"

"I am serious," said Fulumfuchong. "We have abandoned activities on earth for all this while. It may not be save yet for full scale activities to start but I am convinced that it is safe enough for a very small team to go out there and nose round for a few days. I would personally opt to lead this mission and apply all my skills as a blood hound to ferret out information that would be of use to us."

He turned to Mobuh "With your permission sir. I will select a team of spies and go to the earth. I am sure that the solution shall come from there."

"Do you have any specific idea to work on when you go down there?" enquired Itoff.

"Not really," replied Fulumfuchong. "But I am convinced that I will certainly fish out a solution from there."

"What do you others think?" Mobuh asked looking round.

"That is one of the most absurd ideas that have ever been brought up here," said Funkuin. "We have monitors and observe the earth closely everyday. Why would it take Fulumfuchong to go down there before we get good ideas?"

"Your question," replied Fulumfuchong, "is not only ridiculous but stupid. Why does Mungongoh send agents to earth despite the many observatories out here in Mungongoh? Why did you have to send Nyamfuka to earth for your missions if you could simply use the monitor in your office?"

Funfuin was silent.

"Fulumfuchong's suggestion is okay with me," replied Yivissi, "it looks like the only thing to do now. I hope I shall be part of the mission."

"I think I like the idea," said Itoff. "Besides, no other concrete option has surfaced and may not surface before the deadline."

There was a general round of acquiescence.

"Okay," said Mobuh. "Fulumfuchong shall select his team and go to the earth. We understand that he is aware of the urgency of the situation, so we will meet back here immediately he comes back."

Fulumfuchong had always had a crush on Yivissi and her interest in a trip to earth with him gave him some hope that his advances would not be rebuffed. She was the first person on his list of those to accompany him. Then there was the smart looking Apollo called Nyamfuka that Funkuin had colonized, but who could charm any female secretary on earth into cooperating. Nyamfuka was a young handsome agent who had made several missions on earth and knew his way around. Funkuin had used him effectively in one of her strategies where, he was required to slip the neutron bomb formula across to a renowned professor and make it look like he had developed it himself. The process of slipping across the formula involved charming the professor's secretary into cooperating and Nyamfuka had achieved this with much ease. Access into the presence of a president would mean hustling through tight security and stern looking secretaries. Getting the secretaries on your side meant that you cold equally get them to soften up the security.

The other members of the team were chosen for other various reasons, technical or tactical, but Fulumfuchong did not really think that he would need them for his private mission on earth. However, since his mission had to look genuine, he had to take on personnel that would convince Mobuh and Itoff that he was serious. This was certainly a journey of no return for most of the crew members. Finally, the team was complete and prepared to take off for its special mission.

9

The selected crew was bundled into a cream coloured craft that Fulumfuchong himself, who was a senior engineer in aeronautics, had designed. The space craft was equipped with modern communication equipment and lots of intricate gadgets and materials. It had all the comfort that you would find in the best hotels on earth and more. This was supposed to be a special trip so it was made really special. Fulumfuchong had Yivissi that he had long admired on board. He had special plans to woo her successfully and felt it necessary to create the right atmosphere for this. He did not want to be disturbed in the least bit in his wooing effort and was not prepared to take 'no' for an answer. Everything had to be just right.

After a few hours of cruising, Fulumfuchong went into the first part of his plan, which involved getting the first accomplice for the realization of his real plans on earth. The fact that this first target was Yivissi made the prospect more pleasant. As captain of the crew, he had every delicacy in his cabin, even kola coffee. He placed some of these temptingly on the table and invited Yvissi.

"I am pleased to receive the prettiest member of the IRDI in my humble cabin," he said to her as a sign of welcome.

"I would not call this lavish display in this room, humble," replied Yivissi, looking around. "You wanted us to discuss something?"

"Sure!" replied Fulumfuchong. "You are a member of the IRDI and therefore my colleague. The two of us have to work closely for the success of this mission, very close indeed. I think I count myself the luckiest man in Mungongoh for this singular opportunity."

"What opportunity?" asked Yivissi

"The opportunity to work and be close to you throughout this trip," replied Fulumfuchong. "You are very different from all those witches in the IRDI, a rare pearl and an exquisite presence."

"Is there something else on your mind apart from our mission?" Yivissi asked.

Fulumfuchong heaved a sigh of relief. Yivissi had opened the door somehow.

"To be candid," replied Fulumfuchong, "I have always admired you and have always longed for such an occasion where I would sit close to you and declare my ardent desire to make you mine."

"Interesting," said Yivissi and subsided into silence.

This embarrassed Fulumfuchong somehow and for five full minutes he neither knew what to do nor what to say. He would have loosened up however if he had known what was transpiring in Yivissi's mind. Yivissi's silence was not that of scorn. At last, a man was virtually proposing to her. Fulumfuchong could not actually be termed, handsome, but he was a member of the IRDI, which made him a top choice. He was still a bachelor too, and whatever he lacked in looks would be compensated by his intelligence and class. For her part, the beautiful Yivissi had risen quite rapidly under the very protective eye of an influential and stern mother.

Yivissi's mother had propelled her into the glory of being a member of the IRDI but overlooked what is foremost in every woman's mind, marriage. Many handsome young men and men of substance admired Yivissi but lacked the courage to approach her. Her life had thus been full of glory and every nice material thing one could imagine, but devoid of love. She had never really missed that love because she was always busy with her work or her mother and no male had actually approached her to awaken that flame of passion that is lying latent in every woman. Now that Fulumfuchong was clumsily insisting on her womanly virtues, and her work and mother were not there to take up her time, it occurred to her that a woman needs some loving to keep her going.

"Has the ardent desire to make me yours suddenly died down?" Yivissi finally asked.

"Eh?" replied the confused Fulumfuchong.

"It looks like the burning desire for me has petered out." she said, smiling. "Maybe you want me to take over?"

This statement took Fulumfuchong off gear but rekindled the ardour in him, and all his confidence came back. He jumped up from his chair, dragged Yivissi into his arms and kissed her warmly.

Fulumfuchong had finally succeeded in charming Yivissi into accepting his love advances. It would not be difficult now to make her an accomplice in his plans on earth. That was the first conquest. Fulumfuchong's next target was Nyamfuka who would be in a good position to enable them break through formidable defences that always blocked access to presidents. There was also another advantage to be gained in roping in Nyamfuka as an accomplice. He was already mapping out a strategy to overthrow king Awobua and would need every possible support back in Mungongoh. Apart from females on earth, Nyamfuka had equally penetrated the heart of Dr. Funkuin, a powerful female to reckon with and certainly a powerful ally if she could accept to be on your side. He was aware of the fact that to turn Nyamfuka round would be very difficult and needed quite some tact. After deciding on what he thought would be the best approach, he called Nyamfuka to his room.

"I hear you are very close to Dr. Funkuin," he said, smiling roguishly. These guys need to be put at ease when you have something strategic and risky to ask them.

"Kind of," said Nyamfuka smiling back.

"How is she in bed?" Fulumfuchong asked carelessly.

"I wouldn't know sir," replied Nyamfuka without hesitation.

"Don't kid me," Fulumfuchong said, without any animosity. "Everyone knows that you are the lucky fellow she has a crush on. Of course we are aware of her sexual relationship with Itoff, but that is just for power and influence. Are you saying that the crush she seems to have on you has been wasted all this while? She is such an attractive and sexy dame."

"What I mean is that we never had sex in bed," replied Nyamfuka.

"Where then? By the street side?" Fulumfuchong smiled encouragingly.

"Not quite sir. The main problem is that she is often so busy and I am often on mission, so we just have sex wherever we have the chance, and a bedroom has never been available whenever the possibility came up. It often happens in her office toilet and on a few occasions, in other toilets."

"But she has a comfortable home with no husband there to break your neck or batter you into pulp." Fulumfuchong pointed out.

"Itoff suspects my relationship with her and keeps a close eye. I would never be able to sneak into her home without Itoff rushing there and committing havoc."

"And your own home?"

"Itoff watches that too. There is no way Funkuin can come in there without Itoff being immediately informed. I am sure if he were not yet hooked to another woman, he would have married her so he could have the right officially to kill anyone who so much as ogled at her."

In Mungongoh, there were no polygamous marriages but married men were free to flirt with unmarried women. Flirting with a married woman was quite risky because the law gave the cuckolded husband the right to maim or kill any buck who tampered with his wife. In Nyamfuka's case, Itoff had no right to actually inflict bodily harm but since Nyamfuka too was not a legal husband to Funkuin and Itoff was a senior official, Nyamfuka had to be contented with playing second fiddle, and playing to Itoff's tune.

Fulumfuchong was smart to realize that another door had been opened but this time, it was to the delicate task of convincing Nyamfuka to cross to his side.

"And that bloke Itoff is so protected by Mobuh that he could do anything to you and go unpunished," said Fulumfuchong pitifully. "Do you know that those two often accuse a few unfortunate members of the IRDI of treason whenever they want to dispose of them?"

"Ordinary Mungongoh citizens like us are not quite aware of that," said Nyamfuka. "But because Itoff is a very powerful man, my relationship with Funkuin has remained timid."

"There, you are doing the right thing. If Itoff actually catches you in the act, you may not stay alive to tell it to the next man. You know, the heartless blokes accuse innocent Mungongoh citizens of treason, aware of the fact that punishment for such a crime is to be offered as a meal to the lions."

Nyamfuka shivered. He had witnessed this horrible form of capital punishment before but had always joined the others in blaming victims for daring to challenge the king and bring chaos to the country. It had never occurred to him that any of the condemned chaps could have been framed.

"Yes," said Fulumfuchong. "Itoff may be biding his time, but eventually he would find a way of getting you accused of treason and kept out of the way. You see the kind of persons that the king keeps around him?"

Nyamfuka was shocked. He had never heard that type of blasphemous way of talking about the king before. King Awobua was considered as unchallengeable, untouchable and perfect, and was revered by all the people of Mungongoh, and Nyamfuka had never heard anything but praises and adoration showered on the king. From the days of the great clever king who brought them out of Mars, Mungongoh kings have always been worshipped and considered as some kind of God. Their birth was always made mysterious and hidden away from public comprehension by the chief minister and a special nurse retained for the purpose of bringing up the future king. That is why Mungongoh kings never had queens. Heirs were fathered by the king, who had three women to copulate with. As soon as three male offspring were available, one of whom will eventually become king, the three women were sent away from the palace and the kids handed over to the nurse. Although the children grew up in the palace, they were kept away from the people. When the chosen one came up to five hundred years old, he was officially shown to the public, giving the impression that he had just appeared.

"If you are complaining about the king's choice of close collaborators, it means you have doubts about the king. Let me warn you that such licentious talk could land us into serious trouble. We came on a mission to find out the best strategy of making our king ruler of the earth." Nyamfuka was quite stern.

"Don't take it like that" Fulumfuchong realized that he had to tread carefully. He decided to try another approach.

"Do you really love Funkuin?" he asked Nyamfuka.

"She is the best woman I have ever had in Mungongoh. A bit commanding and rather older than me, but fun to be with and loving," replied Nyamfuka.

"So you would like to have her all to yourself, marry her if possible?"

"Very much! The problem now is that she actually gains much from Itoff and is compelled to show gratitude for what he has done for her."

"I rather don't see what he has done that she would not have achieved herself. She is quite an intelligent woman and catches the eye of most of those blokes in the IRDI. What a pity that she thinks that she owes much allegiance to Itoff for her position in the IRDI."

"That is true," said Nyamfuka. "Often, it galls me to hear her praise him unnecessarily."

"Her relationship with him does not bother you?"

"No man wants to see the woman he loves being controlled by another man. But there is nothing I can do because he is very powerful. Besides, Funkuin herself is my boss so I don't have much command over her."

"Would you like to see things reversed?"

"How?" asked Nyamfuka hopefully.

"I mean changed. Itoff's position and power stripped off and you becoming Funkuin's boss."

"How can that work? Itoff is virtually the third most powerful man in Mungongoh and Funkuin is a big professor and member of the highest institution in Mungongoh. I am only a small agent, a junior servant for that matter."

Fulumfuchong surveyed Nyamfuka speculatively.

"We could change things together. We could start from the top."

"But at the top is king Awobua." Shouted Nyamfuka.

"And as long as he is there Mobuh and Itoff will always be there. Funkuin will always be your boss. Your access to her will be limited to taking pot luck in some toilet or washroom. You will never enjoy the position of a dominant boyfriend or husband. Think over it."

"Nyamfuka thought over it. Treason was a terrible thing to be involved in, but Fulumfuchong was right. As long as things remained the same he would never be in the position to claim any rights over Funkuin, and that was his biggest wish.

Fulumfuchong seized this opportunity and continued.

"King Awobua is doing absolutely nothing to develop Mungongoh. The kings before him did much but since he came to the throne nothing has been improved. He spends his whole time dreaming of conquering the earth. Don't you think that this should stop?"

Nyamfuka was confused. Fulumfuchong had a solid point there but he was talking about treason.

Fulumfuchong's droning voice continued

"You have been on the earth as a spy several times. You have seen the nice things they have there. That delicious Kola coffee made by the NWCA in Cameroon, chocolate, bacon, cigars etc. You must have equally noticed their cravings for things that are littered on the hills, valleys and soils of Mungongoh such as diamonds and other stones that are precious to them. You are aware of the fact that the Mungongoh earth crust is full of ores of precious metals like gold and silver. We could sell some of these things to the earth governments and import their delicacies. How I would love to always have Kola coffee and caviar in my home."

Mungongoh was virtually a version of Voltaire's Eldorado. The rocky Mungongoh had much gold and Silva embedded in the crust. There were equally pebbles of diamonds and other precious stones littered all over in some parts of the land. Some of the aquatic creatures in the crater lakes had pearls that the people extracted and carelessly discarded when they wanted to eat the creatures. Since these things did not mean anything to the people of Mungongoh, nobody ever bothered about them.

Fulumfuchong looked at Nyamfuka again. He seemed to be coming round. Fulumfuchong was sure that he was now ready for the real thing

"Have you ever come across a coup d'état during one of your various trips to earth?"

"You mean an uprising?" asked Nyamfuka "I have come across many when operating on earth."

"Not just an uprising," said Fulumfuchong. "A takeover! On earth it is often done by soldiers, who use their guns to take over power from a monarch or a president, or whatever leader they want to dispose of." explained Fulumfuchong.

"Those have been a very normal occurrence in Latin America. In Africa, Ghana and Nigeria are so far the champions. Yes, I think I am well versed with this coup d'état issue, but how does it concern us?"

"We shall have to carry out one in Mungongoh, depose Awobua and take over power."

"You must be joking!"

"I am serious."

"Do we have to do that? It is impossible." Nyamfuka was shaking violently.

Fulumfuchong tried to calm him down.

"Mungongoh is in great danger. Awobua is bent on doing anything to conquer the earth and you very well know that it

71

will not be that simple. The earthlings have many ways of defending themselves and may rather turn around and strike at Mungongoh. Think of the devastation that the king's stupidity might cause," Fulumfuchong said desperately. Nyamfuka was being far more difficult than he had imagined.

"But overthrowing the king," insisted Nyamfuka.

"Consider the number of innocent men that have passed through the jaws and stomachs of his lions, not to talk of the unfortunate dwarfs. What type of king keeps away from his people and has absolute power. You have operated on earth for quite a while don't you think we need some democracy in Mungongoh?"

A silence of uncertainty followed. After about five minutes, Nyamfuka finally broke the silence.

"Okay," said Nyamfuka at last. "Let us say we decide to carry on with this project, how do we go about it? Are you forgetting that the king has ferocious guards in his palace? How do we even get to the king?"

"Leave that to me," replied Fulumfuchong reassuringly. He was speaking with much relieve.

"But what will happen to the king?" Nyamfuka asked

"Should that bother you?" replied Fulumfuchong. "If you must know, we will have to kill him. That is what they do on earth. If the fellow is allowed to stay alive, he will remain a threat. Some dethroned presidents, escape or are exiled to other countries but Mungongoh has no such options."

Nyamfuka remained silent again for a short while and then smiled broadly.

"I suppose this coup d'état thing stretches to Mobuh and Itoff?"

"Certainly! When the king goes, they go."

"Well, here I am struggling to support people who do not give a damn about me. I even have an axe to grind with Itoff. I will go with you all the way."

The other members of the team did not need to be involved until when he was sure his plan will succeed. He was not sure whether they would accept to follow him and thought it was safer to live them out completely. It would even be safer to eliminate them. He could pilot the craft on the return trip.

10

After zooming round the earth twice, Fulumfuchong finally opted for the landing spot close to Bermuda. They had several of such landing spots depending on where they wanted to operate. During the flight Fulumfuchong had not only concentrated on getting accomplices. He had given much thought as to where to start first. He had considered the biggest superpowers, America and Russia, but finally decided that he could not trust the Russians fully. He would go straight to the President of America and convince him about the danger facing the earth. America was the most powerful country and was in a position to provide all the assistance needed or on the other hand, mobilize all the other big countries into action.

After disguising their flying saucer, Fulumfuchong gave the other crew members directives as to what they were supposed to do and get back to the craft in a hurry. He then took Yivissi and Nyamfuka along with him to talk to the President of America.

"What will you tell him?" asked Yivissi

"Anything that could spur him into action," replied Fulumfuchong. He had not revealed his full plan to his colleagues.

"Your choice of America is quite good," said Nyamfuka. "Everybody listens to their powerful president."

To get to the President however was not as easy as he had thought. He had not anticipated the fact that so many people could be deployed just to protect one man. The king of Mungongoh had guards but then they had not been put there to prevent people from being received by the king. For their own good, citizens of Mungongoh were generally not allowed into the presence of their king, but then, he never pretended that he was the servant of the people. Again, the people of Mungongoh had no problems that needed a solution from the king. The guards were there mainly for fancy although they were well trained. In the case of America, the President seemed to be more protected than a high security prison. To get to him was another matter as you had to be screened and convince security experts that your motive for wanting to see the President was important and pure. Besides, you needed an appointment.

When Fulumfuchong and his team introduced themselves as visitors from outer space and specifically from a place called Mungongoh, with an urgent message for the President, the obvious conclusion was that they had a few nuts screwed the wrong way upstairs. Instead of being admitted to see the President, they were roughly taken by the scruff of the neck and thrown out, and advised to go back to whatever asylum they had escaped from. Even the beautiful Yivissi was ruffled with indifference. It was not even possible to get past the guards to the level of the secretaries where Nyamfuka would have come in handy.

"My plans include enlisting for help from this big man and I can't get further than the gates. What do you suggest?" Fulumfuchong said, expecting a god response from Yivissi and Nyamfuka.

"If Mungongoh is considered as of no importance by the earthlings, then tell them we are from Mars or Jupiter. That will sound more impressive." suggested Yivissi who had stuck to her new found sweet heart.

"You think so?" enquired Fulumfuchong.

"I would suggest something else sir." Nyamfuka stepped in. "I have carried out a great number of missions to earth and I think I understand them to an extent. These conceited earthlings believe that they are the only living intelligent creatures in the universe. It does not occur to them in any way that there could be life in other planets, let alone satellites like Mungongoh. They reject your requests to see the President simply because they consider it odd that any sane person would introduce himself as a visitor from outer space. I suspect they conclude that you are demented."

"Fulumfuchong is one of the most level headed persons in Mungongoh." protested Yivissi.

"I suppose so," replied Nyamfuka. "But the earthlings do not know about it. I think we should change our approach."

"What do we do?" asked Fulumfuchong.

"We should rather send Yivissi to charm some of those government officials into accepting to lead us to the President," replied Nyamfuka.

"What does it entail?" Yivissi was looking radiant and charming in her scarlet dress.

"Not quite much," replied Nyamfuka carefully. "You just need to smile sweetly, kiss the official lightly on the chicks if you see that it could help or go further if necessary."

"What do you mean by further?" asked Fulumfuchong suspiciously.

"Many earthlings are lechers and take advantage of every situation," said Nyamfuka. "They may carelessly tap her on the buttocks, squeeze her breasts and even request for a quickie in any nearby toilet. You need to see what happens in most of those private toilets." Nyamfuka was smiling mischievously as Fulumfuchong hugged his sweetheart protectively.

"I will be damned if I allow Yivissi to be pawed by any decadent earthling. Why don't you look for another way out?" he queried

"Let us try Russia then" proposed Nyamfuka. "We may be rejecting just the place that could be of help."

After thinking deeply for a while, Fulumfuchong finally concluded, "Let's go to Russia."

The trio teleported themselves to Russia.

In Moscow, the Kremlin police was even rougher and threatened to put them away for eternity. Exasperated, Fulumfuchong finally turned to Yivissi for comfort.

While stroking his worried brow, Yivissi said, "With all his experience on earth I would think that Nyamfuka should have a store of solutions to this problem."

"I have been thinking hard actually" Nyamfuka admitted "and I think I have an idea."

"Let's hear it," said Fulumfuchong, suddenly perking up.

"Yivissi could be the solution. The big presidents often have female secretaries who secretly rub their tired backs and chests once in a while. Some of these mistresses are even known to provide blow jobs to the top executives."

"I have told you that I will never sacrifice my Yivissi for anything. Get that into you thick skull and no more of that rubbish." Fulumfuchong replied angrily.

"I was rather thinking about me seducing one of these girls," Nyamfuka replied hastily. "But before you get in there to these females, you will find mostly important looking males who think they own the President instead of realizing that he is a public servant."

"You now seem to be suggesting that my delicate Yivissi should offer herself to them in a bid to break through?" Fulumfuchong asked

"But I need Yivissi to soften up the men before I get through to the secretaries." Nyamfuka complained.

"It takes a tough woman to do that." Fulumfuchong said sternly. Yivissi may not know how to go about it and some of those macho men may rather end up exploiting her naivety and ignorance."

"Don't panic," said Nyamfuka. "There is another way out. I think we could still use women but with another approach."

"Say on" encouraged Fulumfuchong, now a bit relieved.

"The Presidents of small African countries would be more approachable. Many of them have concubines who can open the gate to the President, through a simple telephone call. If we locate such a president and his concubines, I could charm a concubine into interceding for the President to receive us."

"This young buck simply wants a chance to sample a few of the African women" laughed Yivissi.

"Possible, but these small presidents with their small countries have no force. We cannot rely on them to carry out our plan. Of what use will that be to us then?" asked Fulumfuchong.

"The small presidents stand a greater chance of being received by the President of the USA than us. If we can convince a small president about the situation and its urgency, it will be easy for him to get us to see the big presidents."

Fulumfuchong thought about it and it made sense. Besides the other options suggested involved Yivissi virtually being used as bait. It would be better to stick to this new idea and hope that it would work.

After thorough analysis of presidents, they settled on the President of Kenya. The Kenyan women had just declared a sex strike to oblige their husbands to fight against certain bad practices in the country. The assumption was that the President would certainly succumb to whatever request a concubine made if there was a reward of sexual gratification, after being starved by his wife for a few days. To bolster the bargaining power of the concubine and enable her to resist giving in to the President prematurely, Nyamfuka would be available to satisfy her sexually during the strike period. Another advantage in the choice of the President of Kenya was that he was the President of the President of America. This may sound confusing but he was the President of the father of the President of America, and in most parts of the earth, you follow your father and not your mother. You even join your mother to adopt your father's name.

The concubine identified was an ebony black beauty called Alice. She was really dashing and so attractive that Fulumfuchong secretly envied Nyamfuka's role. Nyamfuka for his part was so artful that Alice proved quite helpful in getting them to be received by the President.

After receiving Fulumfuchong, the President of Kenya reacted promptly. He got into contact with the US president and succeeded in convincing him to accept to receive Fulumfuchong. The choice of Nyamfuka as an ally was bearing fruits. Fulumfuchong's only worry was that the young hound may eventually apply his charms on Yivissi. He had already noticed that Yivissi had started speaking fondly of Nyamfuka.

Fulumfuchong and his colleagues could have simply teleported themselves to America, but they were compelled to accept the hospitality of the President of Kenya, who offered the Presidential jet for this purpose. The earthling planes were quite slow and made a lot of noise. However, to Nyamfuka's delight, the hostesses were shapely, beautiful and very attentive. This should be hot stuff, he thought.

11

The president of America received them in the White House with a warm and broad smile. For the first time America had a president who somehow was linked in one way or another to various races represented in America and representative of virtually all the continents in the world. He had black and white blood, had been christened with an Arabic name, and was a hero in Indonesia in the Far East. He was more intelligent than most university dons, and looked more like a movie super star whenever he took the rostrum. Fulumfuchong concluded that this was actually the person to handle the crises intelligently.

As the President came into the room where Fulumfuchong was waiting, he eyed the supposed extraterrestrial beings with interest. Fulumfuchong looked very ordinary in his French cut suit. He was sipping and enjoying coffee like any other American. There was nothing in him that smacked of an extra terrestrial. He rather had the looks of a very polite, respectful and intelligent person. His companions were also dressed like regular Americans and did not even look like they had been anywhere out of America.

"Good morning and welcome to America." The President said, smiling.

"I am glad you finally decided to receive us sir" Fulumfuchong replied with a lot of respect.

"Well, if the President of Kenya sent you to me, then it must be important."

The President motioned for them to sit down.

"Where is this planet of yours located and how is it called?" he asked.

"It is a satellite of Mars, just like the moon is a satellite of the earth. It is called Mungongoh and slightly smaller than the moon." Fulumfuchong explained. "You people have been concentrating on Mars and forgetting about anything else."

"This is all very strange," said the President. "But how do you expect me to believe you? What prove have you got that this satellite exists and is inhabited by people who look like us? I have always thought that extraterrestrial's were strange greenish beings, with massive skulls and tiny limbs."

"What an idea!" said Fulumfuchong. "You can see how beautiful our female companion is. What actually gave you the idea about massive skulls and tiny limbs, sir?"

"We generally imagine out here on earth that extraterrestrials have big brains and are very intelligent.' The President said. "With this extra intelligence, they do not need to do any physical work and so do not need powerful limbs."

Nyamfuka, who had much more experience about earthlings, through his various missions to earth, jumped in to help.

"Sir you remember that more than twenty five years back some strange things happened on earth. Dangerous disease samples were disappearing from laboratories. Even dangerous elements like plutonium were sneaked away."

"Yes," said the President trying to recall. "I might have been in High school then and had not even dreamt that I would ever become president. That would have been in the days of Carter, Reagan or some other person. I remember a summit was held out there, somewhere in Africa. What has your presence here got to do with it?"

"I was one of the agents who had been dispatched from Mungongoh to coordinate the stealing of those items. I even succeeded in recruiting quite a number of Americans to work with us." Nyamfuka said.

"How could it be?" asked the President. From your looks you must have been a child then."

"Actually sir, we live longer than you earthlings and as such, age at a far slower pace."

"How is that?" asked the President. "That is hard to believe."

"There is no time to explain all that now sir," said Nyamfuka, "but it is the truth."

The President turned to one of his aides. The aide moved over to the computer terminal by a window, searched for three minutes and announced triumphantly.

"I have it all here sir."

"Then let's hear it," the President said.

"It was about twenty six years ago when president Forest was just one year in office. Nuclear material and specimens of dangerous diseases were disappearing from laboratories and stores. Eventually the FBI apprehended a few culprits whom they assumed should have come from Russia. After thorough investigation it was discovered that they were all called 'Innocent' in a bid to derail our lie detectors. They had all come from a strange place called Mungongoh. Shortly after, it was discovered that quite a number of Americans had been recruited to assist these infiltrators. None of the missing items has ever been found anywhere on earth. President Forest had called a summit of super powers somewhere in Equatorial Africa, where constant alert was recommended. Since then however, no disappearances of any strategic stuff has been recorded."

The President turned to Fulumfuchong.

"You claim that you are from this strange place, whatever you call it?"

"Mungongoh sir, Yes sir," replied Fulumfuchong.

"And why have you come to see me?" the President asked

"The earth is in peril sir. You are the President of the most powerful country on earth. That is why I assumed you are best placed to do something."

"What makes you think that the earth is in peril?"

"Our king, Awobua and his senior minister, Mobuh are bent on conquering the earth."

"What rubbish. Conquer the earth? How do they hope to do that?" the American president asked, perplexed

"You just heard sir that lots of materials for the production of nuclear weapons and lots of samples of dangerous pestilences were stolen some decades back, and no trace of them has ever been found."

"Yes?" the President was in between shock and embarrassment.

"All these things are in Mungongoh and will be used to destroy the inhabitants of the earth."

"But why would they want to destroy the inhabitants of the earth?" asked the American president.

"King Awobua has no other dream but the conquest of the earth. Mobuh his chief minister is bent on giving his king satisfaction and assist him in ruling the earth."

"But that is not possible. There are empty planets like Mars that they could occupy. If you people can survive on a satellite that is similar to the moon, then, you can survive anywhere," the President said.

"They actually mean to annihilate the human race, clear them off completely from the surface of the earth and occupy it."

"What an idea." the President burst out. "Here we are in America compelled to cope with aggressive neighbours, Islamic fundamentalism, autocratic and totalitarian regimes all over the place, and now, a bigger threat comes looming. Why are the chaps Awobua and Mobuh not satisfied with their planet?"

"The situation is urgent sir. We must act fast. Mungongoh is smaller than the moon in size. It has a very rocky surface with very little greenery. We thus have very few animals and very little to eat in terms of food. That is why even every flying or crawling insect constitutes a food item."

The President considered this for a while. He was still not fully convinced that this story was real.

"You are also a citizen of this place?"

"Mungongoh!" Fulumfuchong pointed out. "I suppose you don't even remember my name again."

The President made a mental effort but failed. He then sneaked a look at the disguised console by his side.

"Felumfechoung right?"

"Wrong. Fulumfuchong."

"Okay, whatever the name is, you are a citizen of the aggressive planet and you will certainly benefit from the occupation of the earth by your king, just like the others. Why have you therefore come to us? Are you one of those manipulating traitors who go for money? What do you want from us?" the President was watching him closely.

"I am no traitor. I am working for the good of my people. King Awobua is a tyrant. You cannot imagine how many of us get transformed into snacks for his lions. The king only dreams of conquering the earth, and there is absolutely nothing to show in terms of development since he became king."

"Are you saying that you have no personal ambitions?" asked the President.

"No person grows up and develops without personal ambitions," replied Fulumfuchong. "You became the

President of America because you were ambitious, probably not for wealth and riches, but to implement policies which you are convinced will help the country and the world. I have that kind of ambition. Besides, I am aware of the arsenals you have and your capacity to strike back. Mungongoh may not be spared if war broke out."

For five minutes the President had nothing to say. He was one of the smartest presidents America ever had, but this was quite a delicate issue. It was very difficult to believe in this story of an extraterrestrial threat. Yet if he ignored it and it was real, then his country and the earth will be in peril. One of his predecessors was said to have called for a summit of world powers on this issue. Should he believe in this science fiction story that was unravelling in front of him? He decided on a last probe.

"Why did you pass through the President of Kenya instead of coming straight to me?"

"It was not easy getting in here. We tried but we were rather taken for mad persons. We finally decided to pass through the President of Kenya because we believed that as the son of a Kenyan, you would listen to him."

Fulumfuchong was smart enough to avoid the fact that they had exploited a sex strike and used the President's concubine.

"Suppose we believe your story, what do you expect us to do?" the President asked.

"I was thinking of an action far away from earth," replied Fulumfuchong. "An action that will not even be felt on earth."

The President heaved a sigh of relief. This was a lot better.

"Go ahead." He encouraged.

"We need your assistance to overthrow king Awobua and put an end to all of this."

The President shook his head. Overthrowing established presidents or kings was not what America stood for any longer. Before, because of the fear of the spread of communism, America was often instrumental in the overthrow of established regimes. The communist system had weakened considerably and even disappeared in Europe. At the same time, America had come to realize that in many cases, they had replaced good presidents with monsters like Mobutu. They had thus switched over to the other extreme and were now totally opposed to the overthrow of established governments, even rotten ones like in Zimbabwe. The issue of overthrowing the king of Mungongoh thus pricked him as wrong.

"We don't participate in overthrowing established governments," he said sternly to Fulumfuchong.

"We are not talking about a government on earth" Fulumfuchong pointed out "We are talking about a government away from earth that is threatening the whole world including America. We want to transform a destructive war into a mere overthrow of a bad regime."

After reflecting for a short while the President concluded "Then I must summon another summit of superpowers. There, we can all agree on your authenticity and the steps to take. This is a global problem you know."

Fulumfuchong was exasperated.

"You must do something now sir" he shouted in desperation. "There is very little time. We struggled to get to you because with the support of America alone we can succeed."

The President turned to the aide who had moved closer to him when Fulumfuchong was shouting in desperation, prepared to defend his president in case of violence. "Summon an emergency strategic meeting. It will hold in an hour's time. But first switch on the hotline let me talk to my Russian counterpart."

He turned to Fulumfuchong.

"We will meet back here tomorrow for a concrete decision to be taken. Don't worry; you will be taken to an apartment where you will have every access to food, snacks, entertainment and comfortable beds."

As they moved out to be taken to their quarters, Nyamfuka discretely squeezed the hand of the beautiful American woman who was leading them to their apartment and whispered in her ears "I hope you will join me later in my room"

She smiled sweetly and said nothing.

12

The next day as Fulumfuchong, Dr Yivissi and Nyamfuka were ushered into the Oval office, the President stood up and received them as if they were very high dignitaries. His strategic meeting with his top aides had revealed a lot. A thorough analysis of the summit that had held some decades back proved that Fulumfuchong could actually be genuine and his claims worth taking seriously. The President now had the Secretary of State, the Secretary of Defence and a few top advisers by his side.

"Welcome honourable guests." he said smiling broadly. "I hope you had a good night. Did you enjoy your breakfast?"

Fulumfuchong had enjoyed the sumptuous breakfast. There had been toast, butter, sausages and cheese to be washed down with wonderfully flavoured coffee.

"Thank you for the hospitality sir." He replied, "We have never been treated to such a meal before."

"Okay," said the President satisfied. Here is the Secretary of State for America Mrs. Doomsday and the secretary for defence, General Butcher. Mr. Pugachev and Mr O'Tool are my chief advisers. Mr. Ferret there is the chief of the FBI, while Mr. Mac Intouch here is the chief of CIA."

"Good morning sirs" Fulumfuchong greeted.

"Good morning and welcome," they all replied.

Mr. Ferret was eying Fulumfuchong closely as if he were looking for a clue to prove that Fulumfuchong was the devil.

"Sit down lady and gentlemen," said the President. "Let us go ahead and see what we can do about this peril that we are facing."

He turned to Fulumfuchong "I think we are convinced that you are telling the truth."

89

"Where is Mungongoh?" asked the Secretary for Defence. "You realize we can't do much if we don't quite know who is threatening us."

Fulumfuchong put up his hand.

"Not so fast. First, we agree on what I want you to do, then, I tell you where Mungongoh is."

"I hope you did not come here to dictate to us," said the secretary for defence angrily. "This is mighty America."

"It is mighty America on Earth but not where Mungongoh is concerned." retorted Fulumfuchong. "Besides what I want to do would be helpful to both of us. Apart from peace and the safety of the earth, I am looking at mutual trade. Mungongoh needs much of what you have in abundance."

"And what shall we have in return?" demanded the President "You know that your money would certainly be useless here."

"True!" replied Fulumfuchong. "But we have much gold, diamond and other shiny stones that you people kill each other for."

All the Americans were immediately very interested. There is nothing that attracts the attention of a capitalist than the prospect of making money. Fulumfuchong immediately noticed the awakened interest.

"Instead of fighting each other and destroying as much as can be done by each side, we could rather engage in something that would benefit both of us."

"How do we go about achieving this lofty idea?" asked the chief of CIA.

"We have to overthrow King Awobua," said Fulumfuchong. "You people have been doing it in African and Latin American countries. I am sure you have quite some experience in knocking off presidents."

"We are not talking about an African country. We are talking about some damned planet we know nothing about." The Secretary of State shouted.

"No problem," said Fulumfuchong. "We just have to agree that you assist me in overthrowing Awobua and I take his place. Then as king of Mungongoh, I would declare peace and open up trade with the Earth. Why, a few tourists from here could visit Mungongoh once in a while."

"Now" requested the secretary for defence calmly "tell us where this Mungongoh is."

"Mungongoh is not quite far off," replied Fulumfuchong. "It is a satellite of Mars. You have probably seen it in your observatories although you have instead been concentrating on Mars to see whether it is inhabitable. Our situations are reversed. Your moon has no life but in our case, our planet has no life."

There was a murmur of surprise throughout the congregation. None of them could have ever imagined that there could be life on a small satellite. Stories about flying saucers had made headlines, but no extraterrestrial being had ever been seen.

"It is easy to fly a few mercenaries to Congo or Uganda. But for your case, how do you expect us to get to Mungongoh?"

"We have flying saucers. That is how we came here."

"If you have that type of advanced technology, then you must have an army that is armed with sophisticated weapons. How do you propose we defeat them?" asked the Secretary for Defence.

"We don't actually have soldiers in Mungongoh. We have never had any wars. Never has there been an attempt to overthrow a monarch. We therefore have never developed weapons, because we have no use for them. King Awobua's guards use physical force to protect him if necessary, but there has never been need for that."

"That is interesting," said the President. "How do they intend to conquer the earth then?"

"They intend to use a combination of weapons we developed only for use on earth," replied Fulumfuchong. "I thought I had told you earlier that king Awobua intends to take over the earth, not to destroy it. His only intention is to clear all humans from the surface of the earth."

"I remember some of the items that were taken so many years ago were intended to make nuclear weapons." The chief of FBI said.

"Actually," replied Fulumfuchong, "the neutron bomb was developed in Mungongoh. It is Nyamfuka who introduced the formula through professor Small's secretary into the professor's papers. Our intention at the time was to push you to use it against each other since we assumed that Russian spies would soon steal the formula to Russia. World war based on the neutron bomb would have annihilated all of you and left the earth for us. Right now in Mungongoh, a few bombs are being developed to be used for the destruction of the earth."

The President took a deep breath and looked round at his colleagues.

"Are you saying you have enough bombs there to kill all of us on earth?" he asked

"Not really," replied Fulumfuchong, to the relief of everybody. "Mungongoh has very little traces of uranium and can only use what they succeed in stealing from the earth. However, you will remember the Fire plague that struck the earth sometime ago?"

All of them were not born at that time, but the devastation had been so horrible that it figured very prominently in all world history books.

"This pestilence" continued Fulumfuchong "was developed in Mungongoh and sent down through a few rats. You earthlings are very smart and somehow managed to put a halt to it. Other pestilences like the bird and the swine flue, the Ebola and what you call AIDS were equally developed in Mungongoh, but had less success than the plague."

"So that is the great danger that has been looming over the earth all this while?" the President asked.

"Yes Even the devastating Spanish flue that made the world wars look like Child's play, were produced in Mungongoh and introduced here. The earth has only been saved by the fact that we lack enough raw materials to operate with."

"But how do we assist you in overthrowing this Awobua then?" asked the CIA chief.

"Get a few tough men to join me on my return trip. Fortunately, I personally designed the flying saucer on which we arrived, I am a senior engineer in aeronautics and could develop a blue print of the craft that brought us here, and give to your scientists. With luck they could succeed in building one or two that could be used for a back up team. In Mungongoh, your guns may be useless, but your soldiers are well trained and know how to fight. Simple brute force is enough for the overthrow effort. The king's guards use truncheons and nobody else is allowed to carry them. Your soldiers can use fists and booted feet, as well as any blunt objects with which violent blows can be administered. They can then move in and grab the king."

"What about the population of Mungongoh? Won't they defend their king?" the Secretary for Defence asked.

"They fear him but deep inside, I think they hate him very much," replied Fulumfuchong. "Nobody will take the extra trouble of defending him apart from his guards."

"And what if the king is not in his palace at the specific moment our troops rush in?" asked the Secretary of State.

"King Awobua never leaves his palace except to go and admire his lions, while they feast on a few innocent victims."

"I am still worried about the population. I am not sure they would allow aliens to come in and rough handle their king," the President said.

"They all hate him. The problem is that they are scared of him and it has never occurred to anyone that he could be overthrown. I assure you that we shall go in like heroes."

"Where is the craft of yours?" asked the President

"Somewhere off Bermuda in one of our secret landing spots."

"You will have to take us there then," said the Secretary for Defence.

"By the way, are there any other crew members?" asked the Ferret.

"Yeah," replied Fulumfuchong. "I was almost forgetting about them. Luckily enough, I dismantled a small part from the craft to prevent them from living without us. The pilot is with them."

"Are they aware of what we have just discussed?" asked the CIA chief

"No!" replied Fulumfuchong. "This is a delicate issue and I could not quite trust them"

"We have to knock them off then," declared the CIA chief "No risks are allowed"

"No problem," replied Fulumfuchong. "When we get there, your men will snuff the life out of them, but you

94

should not let my colleagues see it. They are still soft hearted."

13

The trip back to Mungongoh was prepared with care. Twenty five marines were selected for their capacity to wield heavy objects while moving very fast, and for their capacity to endure. It was decided that Nyamfuka would be left behind as main link during the process and to lead the backup team that would follow shortly as soon as the other flying saucers were constructed. Nyamfuka did not mind staying back for a while longer, given the prospects of nice food and beautiful girls. He had a long briefing meeting with Fulumfuchong, during which all items in their plan were reviewed in detail and any possible short-comings, eliminated.

Top American engineers who had been occupied with updating the space shuttle were redeployed to carry out a thorough inspection of the flying saucer, under the expert guidance of Fulumfuchong. Using a copy of the blue print he had brought along, he explained closely the functioning of the craft, the structure and body work, maintenance aspects, and anything considered important. The American professors took notes and marvelled at the advanced technology displayed in front of them. One difficult aspect was fuel. To achieve speed that was faster than light, the Mungongoh scientists used a certain rock fuel found only in Mungongoh. Since Fulumfuchong had not brought any along, it meant that an alternative fuel had to be considered. Nuclear power was closest but did not seem to be good enough.

After the practical classes on Flying saucer construction, Fulumfuchong's team took off at a speed faster than light on their perilous journey. The soldiers were all tough guys who had been on many difficult assignments, but these had been assignments on earth. This one was quite different, they neither knew where they were going to nor what they would find out there. Nothing had been said about the return trip to earth, making them feel like one of those suicide bombers or kamikaze pilots on a journey of no return. During the flight, Fulumfuchong and Yivissi were kept quite busy. Any information about Mungongoh that the soldiers considered important had to be given and explained where necessary.

After a tense flight, the craft finally landed at the earth port in Mungongoh with its load of coup plotters. To the surprise of the soldiers, it was empty, with no stern looking policemen checking documents or clever looking custom officials scanning through luggage. Fulumfuchong did not expect policemen at the airport but knew that there were supposed to be a few earth port officials and cleaners. The absence of any activity at the earth port thus struck him as odd. But they had already landed and must continue on their mission. He led the soldiers to the earth port car park where several cars were parked.

In Mungongoh, you did no have to own a car or any means of transportation, the things were parked at all strategic areas and if you needed one, you simply used it. The only limit was the choice of vehicle. Certain types were reserved for members of the IRDI. Other classes could use vehicles that corresponded to their ranks. The simplest ones were for the commoners. The cars were constructed such that they did not need any fuel to run, yet, they were capable of achieving speeds that our cars on earth could find impossible to attain. They floated slightly above the ground, making the ride quite smooth.

Fulumfuchong quickly showed the smart soldiers who had been trained on earth to drive anything, ranging from airplanes to boats and trains, how to drive the vehicles. Each person piloted one and followed close behind Fulumfuchong, who led them to King Awobua's palace. As they disembarked and moved into the palace, something struck Fulumfuchong as not normal. There were no ferocious guards daring any entrance into the palace. He moved on with his team stealthily, but unchallenged, and finally came to the king's chambers. The gold plated doors were closed but not locked. However, since the habit of such crack forces is to break in, they jammed open the door with booted feet and jumped in. The king was sitting at the far end of the room smiling.

"Welcome," he said. "I know you came all the way for me. Now, come and get me. I am all yours."

The marines all entered the room, with Fulumfuchong placing himself safely around the middle of the group. When all the intruders had passed through the massive door, it closed and locked on its own.

"I am disappointed at you Fulumfuchong," the king said, still smiling sarcastically. "Such a prospective young rising star turned traitor. Do you realize it is high treason collaborating with your country's enemies? What sort of strong ambition could have driven you to imagine that you could replace me as king? Kings in Mungongoh are born. The position can never be taken by usurpers."

The marines rushed to apprehend the king as he reached out for a switch by the side. They were stopped half way by a glass surface. The king was sitting inside a glass cocoon and totally out of reach. He pressed the switch and the room was suddenly filled with some fowl smelling gas and within a minute the mutineers were lying down unconscious.

When Fulumfuchong got up, his head was throbbing violently. He was lying on the cold floor of the store that was used to preserve food items for the lions. Apart from a small window there was very little else in terms of ventilation. What a terrible end. Fulumfuchong thought. Just then the door creaked open and Ngess stepped in. Since the king often summoned him when everything had gone wrong, he was allowed to go anywhere he wished. He pulled a stool and sat down.

"You are lucky that there were many of you otherwise you would be fed to the lions shortly. However, you still have a bit of time as the king has declared that you should be the last to be thrown in to the beasts," he said.

"How did I get here?" Fulumfuchong was filled with fright.

"You tried to do a very foolish thing, so you were apprehended and brought here. All of you have been condemned to be eaten by the lions, so that is why you are lying in this store," replied Ngess.

"Between us Ngess, do you really believe that trying to destitute the king is wrong?"

Ngess closed the door firmly. He lowered his voice and said, "Wanting to depose a dictator and a very bad monarch is a noble thing. What made the whole thing stupid is the way you attempted to do it."

Fulumfuchong was confused. Some sleazy fellow must have betrayed him. Could it be Nyamfuka or Funkuin his sweetheart? He had made sure throughout while they were on earth, that the other members of the crew suspected nothing. He had kept constantly in touch with them, giving one excuse or another for their delay in returning to the craft. They had remained ignorant about his plans until when they were eliminated prior to take off from the earth, replaced by the human team.

"What did I do wrong?" he asked Ngess.

"You totally ignored the fact that the king's favourite pastime is watching the earth. When you left for the earth, he did not trust you completely. When you started struggling to see the big presidents he watched even more closely and turned up his loud speakers to the loudest. Every word or whisper you uttered on earth was registered by him. If he had a trial court like they have on earth, he would have proven you guilty beyond doubt."

"What should I do now? For such a noble course you people should join hands and save me." pleaded Fulumfuchong.

"Nobody would have the guts to do that," replied Ngess. "You must have seen the shock on their faces when they heard that somebody had dared to overthrow the king. They hate him no doubt, but you can't count on any of them for help."

"You are the only one therefore who is left. Do something." Fulumfuchong was desperate.

"I understand you have some ambition in all this," Ngess said calmly. "You want to be king I am sure. What is in it for me? We are all ambitious you know."

"Just anything you wish," said Fulumfuchong. Then a sudden thought occurred to him. "You know you can be a lot better in that position than Mobuh."

Ngess jumped up in surprise. He wanted a better place in his life and a position where his opinion would be considered, but never in his dreams had he imagined himself in the very high position that Mobuh was occupying.

"You would give me Mobuh's position if I helped you?" he inquired.

"Why not?" replied Fulumfuchong. "You are far more intelligent than him and you would be my saviour."

"Now, where did you leave the rest of the members of your crew?"

"They were all eliminated apart from Dr. Yivissi and Nyamfuka with whom I carried out my plan on earth," replied Fulumfuchong.

"I wonder who this Nyamfuka would be," said Ngess. "I don't think I know him. Where is he? I have not seen any other Mungongoh man among the prisoners."

"I left him on the earth," said Fulumfuchong.

"I hope he has all his communication systems on him. But then, I am not a member of the IRDI, so my simple telephone cannot call him out there," Ngess said standing up. "Your rescue can only be programmed from earth. None of these Mungongoh stooges would know what to do."

"I left Nyamfuka behind for the purpose of leading a back up team here. Unfortunately, my special phone has been confiscated. Look for Dr. Yivissi and get her to contact Nyamfuka."

"That is not possible. She too is waiting to have her turn with the lions. Both of you have been programmed for last, so you still have about two weeks to live," replied Ngess.

Fulumfuchong felt like bashing his head against a wall. "I have led that sterling character into trouble. What have I done?" he moaned.

"We have one last option," he said to Ngess. "We can try Funkuin."

"Funkuin?" asked the astonished Ngess "but everyone knows the degree of antipathy between you and her. Why Funkuin?"

"I know Funkuin does not like me. She will rather see me torn to shreds by ravenous beasts. What I am counting on is the crush she has on this fellow, Nyamfuka. She would certainly be missing him now. I am aware of the fact that her antipathy for me must have reached uppermost heights, as she certainly blames me for Nyamfuka's demise. However her longing to have him back may compel her to link you to him. Being a member of the IRDI, she has our special phone."

It was not easy getting Funkuin to help. Ngess took two hours during which he employed tact and cajoling. He blamed Fulumfuchong in no uncertain manner for having put a promising young man's life in peril, then turned around and told her how they needed only a small phone call to change things. He, Ngess knew what to tell Nyamfuka and guide him to an escape route from the earth.

Ngess finally made his call. When he gave Nyamfuka a thorough picture of what had happened, the young man was furious. When he further informed him it was Funkuin who had enabled him to call, the young man was filled with longing. He asked Ngess to leave everything in his hands. He would know what to do.

Americans are very enterprising people. They have been known to spend billions of dollars only to go to the moon and bring back some useless pieces of rock. The idea of a place in outer space, where there was life, had stirred them into action. They had made space crafts before and even sent some to Mars, but these were not fast enough. Now, they had the blue print of the latest Mungongoh flying saucer left behind by Fulumfuchong. He had personally shown them how the whole thing was constructed and how it worked. The American engineers had set to work and were already achieving something.

After the distress call from Ngess, Nyamfuka immediately went into contact with the President and told him everything. He gave him the urgency of saving Fulumfuchong who would make a better king than Awobua. The President was quick to act and summoned another strategic meeting.

14

During the next strategic meeting the CIA chief proposed the possibility of abandoning Fulumfuchong to his plight instead of taking a risk to save him. Nyamfuka could still make a good king, he insisted.

"Becoming the king makes you a prisoner," replied Nyamfuka. "You may acquire power with the position, but you lose all the fun in life. You cannot even sneak into some shady corner and have an affair without the whole nation hearing about it."

"There is a lot to being a president," said the chief executive of America. "As president, you are number one, the most important and most respected person in the country. Even your wife becomes a first lady although she may be clumsy and dull. I am simply lucky that I have a striking spouse."

"But you have to be interested first and be charismatic and smart. That is why you earthlings have had many bad leaders, simply because they were imposed upon the people or seized power by force even though they are close to nonentities. No! I won't go in for something I know I cannot handle."

After Nyamfuka declined very strongly they decided to follow the plan he had given them.

"But you can propose someone else. Why waste time and take a lot of risk trying to release this man who is certainly being well guarded?" asked the CIA chief.

"We guard only the king in Mungongoh. Condemned persons are simply well locked up. Nobody attempts to rescue them. The fact that a few people are intervening on behalf of Fulumfuchong means that he is considered the right choice, and I think so too," said Nyamfuka.

He was surprised at the attitude of the Americans who claimed that they were prepared to fight to any extreme to protect democracy. Then a thought struck him. American soldiers too were involved and about to be eaten by ravenous beasts.

"I suppose you don't care about your soldiers who went with Nyamfuka," he said. "Is that how easily you give them up?"

"Don't take it like that," replied the CIA chief. "We always do everything to get our soldiers on mission, safely back home. Anyway, you will guide the crack force such that they don't miss the right targets."

The Secretary for Defence took over.

"Mr. President, in two days, one of the flying saucers we have been working on should be ready. We did not know that we would need it so soon but we started working on it immediately Fulumfuchong left."

He turned to Nyamfuka. "How long will it take to go Mungongoh? I hope you guys shall be able to get there on time, otherwise it would be a wasted trip."

"Our experienced pilots take about three days from here to Mungongoh. Your inexperienced pilots will certainly take longer."

"Our pilots are quick to learn," said the Secretary for Defence.

"Maybe," said Nyamfuka. "But your fuel is not the best and I doubt whether it will propel the craft at the required speed. However, give and take, I suppose we shall get to Mungongoh in about ten days. In this case I only hope we will succeed in getting there before it is too late."

"You know that our men need to train a bit before takeoff," said the Secretary for Defence.

"I thought they were chosen because they are already well trained," replied the anxious Nyamfuka. "There is very little time. Anyway, some drilling can take place today and tomorrow, while the technicians are putting final touches on the craft."

Nyamfuka worked with the selected crack force for one whole day, while the engineers were giving the last touches to the flying saucer. The machine looked quite elegant and had cost ten times the amount of money that the latest space shuttle would cost.

The special rock that served in Mungongoh as fuel for the flying saucers was not available on earth. Just a kilogram of this rock was enough fuel to take a space craft to earth and back. In the absence of this rock, a complicated and expensive system was developed, an improvement to the space shuttle nuclear propulsion system.

15

The trained Americans, fifty of them boarded the strange craft, not knowing whether they would ever return to earth. On the other hand, there was quite some excitement as the young heroes anticipated adventure and glory. There had been much crying the day they were taken away from their homes for preparation, as their loved ones were not told where they were heading to. It was a special mission and kept very secret. The press to which a bit of information concerning strange beings and a possible mission to an unknown planet had been leaked was doing everything to get information, but was kept at bay. Security had never been tighter.

Nyamfuka was sitting with the pilot and waiting for takeoff, as soldiers were bustling all over the place arranging their things. This was a hastily built craft for soldiers and lacked all the comfort that was in the original one that Fulumfuchong and his team had taken off in. Everybody thus tried to make himself comfortable in his own way. Nyamfuka was clutching his special communication equipment in his hands. His conversation with Ngess had spurred him to a great extent. The main problem there was the position of Funkuin. She might have assisted Ngess to communicate with him, but her stance would certainly change if she knew what the whole mission was about. Yet, for the mission to succeed he needed to communicate with some trusted person inside Mungongoh. Ngess had given him a vivid picture of the whole scenario. He knew exactly where Fulumfuchong was held prisoner. On the other hand he did not know whether Mungongoh would be anticipating any attack from earth and whether the earth port would be heavily protected against intruders. In desperation he decided to try his charm on Funkuin and lure her into giving him needed information

Funkuin's phone buzzed and her heart leapt as she noticed that it was a call from her special agent Nyamfuka.

"Where are you sweet heart? How are you? In what mess did this horrid Fulumfuchong land you? Are you a prisoner to those dashed earthlings? Ooh my sweetie," she cooed and would have kept cooing like a turtle dove that is receiving a long lost mate back to the nest, if the artful Nyamfuka had not thought it wise to show greater concern.

"I have missed you dear. What has kept me going is the constant hope that you will always be there to receive me. But now, that devilish Fulumfuchong abandoned me here because I refused to join his outrageous attempt to overthrow our gracious king."

Nyamfuka was aware of the fact that apart from the king's guards, there was no secret police who apply hectic methods to extract information from suspects. He was sure that Fulumfuchong had been summarily sentenced to the champing jaws of the lions without any prosecution magistrates or well paid lawyers competing to prove him guilty or not guilty. It was therefore clear that his actual position had not been revealed. But he needed to create an uncertain situation and through that, extract information from Funkuin.

"Sweet heart, although you are my boss, at this dire moments I am taking the risk to express my love to the fullest. Dear, save me."

"I would do anything to save you if only I knew how." Funkuin replied hastily. "I have discovered that you are the man of my life. Itoff will mean nothing to me now apart from being my boss."

"Dearest," said Nyamfuka wearily to play more on her heart "Although I am fully innocent, you know the ways of Mungongoh. The king and the high officials will find it difficult to believe that I am not an accomplice of Fulumfuchong, given the fact that I was part of his mission to earth."

"That is true," she admitted "although I had rather thought that he had eliminated all of you."

"I would have been eliminated like the others if I had not been smart," replied Nyamfuka. "I played along as if I was with him, but in the end he discovered that I was against his intensions when I was obliged to take my stand. Using my knowledge of the earth, I escaped and hid and he abandoned me. My experience about the earth gathered from previous missions on earth has contributed wonderfully in enabling me to escape from the grasp of Fulumfuchong."

"You should have communicated with me immediately." shouted the anguished Funkuin. "What made you sit like a dumb fool and allow that fellow to use you like that?"

"Throughout his stay on earth, the foxy Fulumfuchong made sure all our phones were kept by him. When he was leaving, he abandoned the phone along with my belongings. He had arranged for my immediate arrest before taking off and was thus very certain that I would never have access to the communication device. I was consequently arrested by the earthlings, who took along the communication device together with my things," replied Nyamfuka.

"Then how did Ngess's call to you go through?" She asked rather suspiciously "Don't forget that he used my phone."

"Yeah, that call helped," replied the clever Nyamfuka. "When the blip sounded, those earthling blood hounds did not know what to make of it, so they handed it to me and did

111

not bother to take it back afterwards. They have handsets and walkie talkies but these are all very inferior to our phones."

"Okay then," said Funkuin. "What can I do to help?"

"What is it like, out there?" asked Nyamfuka

"What do you mean?"

"The general atmosphere! I hope Fulumfuchong is no longer a threat. I remember he came across with a bunch of well trained earthling soldiers. Are they all waiting for the lions to put an end to their miserable lives, or are they now in command?"

"They are now under the custody of the lion tenders, waiting to be mauled to death," replied the unsuspecting Funkuin. "They would have been fed to the lions already but for the fact that the king is planning for an elaborate public display."

"What do you mean?"

"As you know, such a thing as an attempt to destitute the king, has never happened in Mungongoh. The king intends to impress upon every one that treason will never work in Mungongoh so the plan for their execution is quite elaborate."

"I am interested even from this distance," said Nyamfuka. "It looks like I will miss a grand show."

"Then hasten to come by whatever means"

replied Funkuin "Are you sure you will ever be able to come back?"

"It all depends. When I was coming down, I brought some pieces of shiny rock which the earthlings lust for so much. I may be able to work with some earthlings and transform one of their spacecrafts. The only problem now would be the earth port in Mungongoh. If it is now heavily guarded, I may never be allowed to land."

"Are you sure an earth craft can ever be transformed to move like our flying saucers?" said the alarmed Funkuin.

"Not to worry," replied Nyamfuka calmly. "When the craft is ready, I will lure all of them inside and take off with them. Then it will be easy to eliminate them out here when we land."

"How ingenuous!" Funkuin was clapping despite her sorrow.

"The only problem would be the earth port in Mungongoh." insisted Nyamfuka.

"I don't see any problem there during our big display of the king's powers," Funkuin replied. "The king intends this grand public display to last for about fifteen days. Each day, the king himself will preside over the feeding of the lions during which two of these earthlings will be fed to the lions. The grand finale would be Fulumfuchong and that his stupid female accomplice, Yivissi."

"But what has that got to do with the safety of landing at the port?" Nyamfuka asked uncertainly "You know that there is no use making all the efforts to get into your loving arms just to end up manhandled by zealous guards at the earth port."

"I have told you there is no danger" Funkuin said. "Just come."

"That is not convincing at all," replied Nyamfuka. "If there is no concrete way out of that danger, I would prefer to stay back and relax in the arms of these beautiful earthling females."

Funkuin jumped up "Don't let me hear about any other woman again or I will cut off that sharp instrument of yours. Take off for Mungongoh as soon as it is possible."

She frowned at the thought of him wallowing on earth in the arms of some blasted females. "The earth port will be free. You know that the king virtually never ventures out of his palace. For the period that he will preside over the execution of the coup plotters, everything else is supposed to stop. No schools, no hospitals, no guards. Everybody will have holidays during that period except the king's personal guards. You will be able to sneak in conveniently and I will hide you until I prove your innocence beyond doubt. Then, we would live happily ever after."

16

King Awobua emerged from his palace moved to the waiting coach. It had been close to a hundred years since he had emerged from his palace for ceremonial reasons. His lions were kept in huge cages within the confines of the palace. The few times he went to admire them eat did not take him out of the palace grounds therefore.

King Awobua was bent on making this occasion memorable. He was dressed in a flowery marked and specially designed robe, crowned with an elaborate colourful cap with tassels. His sandals were of raw leather made from lion skin. The coach took him through cheering crowds for over two kilometres to the venue of the event. Holidays meant no work and no personal occupation. Those who could not have access to the slaughter grounds were compelled to stay in the streets and show maximum support to the king.

Because of the grandeur of the occasion, the culprits were not simply dropped into the lions' cages in the palace grounds. They had rather transferred all the lions some distance away to the appropriate venue for such a grand butchery. The ceremonial ground was something similar to the Circus Maximus in the days of Caesar and ancient Rome. A thunderous applause erupted as king Awobua entered and everybody stood up, and this continued till the king sat on his special place reserved for him. Dwarfs rushed up and down, making sure he was comfortable and that his *mukal* was served and other needs were provided.

"The king of Mungongoh." announced Mobuh who was ensconced in another special place next to the king. "People of Mungongoh, we have been living in peace for all this while ruled by a gentle, understanding and generous king. It is certain that you could never have a better person to rule you."

This announcement was received with lots of clapping and shouting. Finally, the applause died down as the king put up his right hand.

"My worthy subjects," he said.

He did not need to shout. With improved technology, the king's cloths could transmit his speeches far and it would sound as if he was speaking to you from close up.

"Kings of Mungongoh have always been great men. They are born as kings and no ordinary man can become one. Great kings like us should rule over vast domains and my appetite for this big fertile planet called earth is no secret to you all. You are therefore aware of my intention to clear off all those worthless fellows from there and provide a wonderful place for all of you. This means you would have access to all the good things that those greedy pigs on earth gobble up every day. You can see the wonderful future I have been planning for you all this while. Everybody in Mungongoh should be grateful for the efforts I have been making. I even set up an institute of well paid members just so that they should develop ideas to enable us take over the earth. So far the members of the IRDI have not succeeded in coming out with that wonderful idea, but as forgiving as I am, I held back the compulsion of offering them to my lions. Instead of being grateful for this, my leniency was taken for weakness and one of the members of this institution that I had created to enable me take over the earth, rather decided to turn traitor. Whatever the earthlings offered him, I don't know. He allied with earthlings to capture and transform us into slaves. You may have never seen slaves in Mungongoh, but on earth it is quite common."

There was a general display of support for the king. When Fulumfuchong was brought out for all to see the anger that was directed towards him by the crowd was terrible. Dr Yivissi looked very miserable by his side. The tough American soldiers were also brought out for all to see their strange dressing intrigued the ordinary citizens of Mungongoh who had never had any links with anything out of Mungongoh.

"See how miserable they look" announced the king "and anybody who thinks he can betray Mungongoh and its king will end in the same way. The lions will chase them around inside the arena before tearing their flesh and shattering their bones in front of all of us. We shall start with the foreigners, two each day. Fulumfuchong and his partner in crime, Yivissi will be served last. The lingering taste of their flesh will keep my beasts longing for more. Any other traitor will therefore be devoured by them with much relish."

The king turned to Mobuh. "Now let us have the spectacle for today. Select the first two and send in the lions."

Mobuh gave instructions, and Fulumfuchong and Yivissi were taken away. Two Americans were held back by royal guards while the others were removed from the arena. The Americans looked round for a means of escape as the guards left the arena and closed every access. They were well trained and quite tough but the desperation and fright on their faces was very evident as four hungry lions were released into the arena. The lions roared loudly in anticipation of a sumptuous meal and rushed towards the condemned Americans. Their shrieks were terrifying as the lions pounced and mauled them. After knocking the life out of them and the crescendo in the whole spectacle had passed, the lions settled down to their meal. The tough belts and leather boots of the Americans proved a challenge to the lions who had always consumed their meals of dwarfs or Mungongoh citizens, without such obstructions. However the human flesh was salty and thus tastier, so the small inconvenience did not quite matter. As the lions were having their meal, the king turned happily to Mobuh.

"My lions are certainly having a wonderful time. Those beefy earthlings have real muscles not useless flab like you and most of your colleagues". One of the lions dived into the rib cage of one of the corpses and pulled out the lungs along with the entrails.

"Have you ever seen a lion smiling?" the king asked Mobuh.

"No sir," he replied stiffly. The gory scene in front of him was going to knock off his appetite for the day.

For his part, the king was enjoying himself thoroughly.

"That lion over there is definitely smiling," he said, pointing at the beast that had just gobbled up the lungs of its victim and was now going for the heart. Its bloody jowls actually gave the impression that it was smiling with pleasure.

17

Funkuin had a cool shower, wiped her body dry and stood naked in front of the large mirror in her room.

She examined her firm breasts carefully, then diverted her attention to her shapely waist and her hips. Yes, she still had quite a good shape, fit enough for the young Nyamfuka. She smiled at her image in the mirror and picked up a comb lying on a stool by the mirror. Her hair was equally gorgeous.

. She was prepared to risk any consequences and make her life with Nyamfuka, and Nyamfuka had declared his love for her openly and full of passion. That was full proof that he cared for her very much and would happily accept to be hers for ever if he came back. Their bond would even be stronger if she were the one to help him get back to Mungongoh. But would he ever be able to make it back to Mungongoh? Funkum had never been to the earth but she was aware of the fact that their space craft were less efficient. They had actually managed to send a few astronauts to the moon just next door to them and an unmanned space craft further to Mars, but it took an awful lot of time to get there. Would Nyamfuka actually be able to upgrade a space vessel on earth that would be capable of bringing him safely to Mungongoh? Yet, he sounded so hopeful.

Mungongoh was becoming unbearable without Nyamfuka. The king's gory pastime to which all of them of the IRDI had been provided front seats was quite repulsive. The shrieks of the earthlings as they were torn to shreds by the king's lions lingered eerily on in her ears late into her lonely nights while the old Itoff certainly snored blissfully by his wife. That old Itoff will have to be dumped.

Just then her phone rang. She picked it up and was pleased to see that it was Nyamfuka calling.

"Hello dear." she answered

"My darling, I am on my way."

"What do you mean?" Funkum asked perplexed.

"I mean that I am on my way to Mungongoh and your warm arms," replied Nyamfuka.

"On your way to Mungongoh?" asked Funkuim "Please, I am already suffering a lot from your absence. You will only make it worse by kidding me. Are you really coming? So soon, but how can it be? You are not really kidding me, are you?"

"Has the fire for me died?" joked Nyamfuka. "When there is love there is always a way."

"But it is unbelievable, a very pleasant surprise but difficult to believe. How did you get a good craft so fast in that primitive world?"

"I will tell you when I come. Just be prepared to receive me," said Nyamfuka.

"I only hope the vehicle is safe. I don't trust anything made by earthlings. They are so backward."

"Don't worry darling," said Nyamfuka. "I made sure that the vehicle was space worthy before lake off."

"You mean you have already taken off for Mungongoh? asked Funkum with a lot of joy in her voice."

"Yes, I had a smooth take off," replied Nyamfuka.

"Do you know how long it will take you to get here? I shall wait for you at the Earth port," said the lover girl.

"I am sure in the next five days we shall be landing in Mungongoh" Nyamfuka decided not to let her know that they had been travelling for several days already.

"When we get close, I will call so that you will know the exact time and fetch me at the earth port. Remember you promised to keep me hidden until you have guaranteed my safety.

"Sure. I will be there," replied Funkuin hotly.

"What of Ngess?"

"What about Ngess?" Funkuin asked.

"I succeeded in getting this craft workable because of some bits he gave me. You know he is a very intelligent fellow," replied Nyamfuka carefully. "I will need to talk to him to be able to manoeuvre this craft right to Mungongoh. Please help connect me to talk to him."

"I did not know that Ngess knew anything about the earth. You are rather the one who has been going there often. Besides, he knows nothing about even our crafts. Where does he fit in here?"

"Your IRDI was always failing because you people were too conceited to use the ideas of a common man. I tell you, Ngess knows virtually everything, and he understands those space vessels more than most pilots and engineers."

"Ok, I will link you to him, maybe tomorrow," replied Funkuin. "Just take good care of yourself. I want you back in one piece."

"Don't worry darling," replied Nyamfuka. "For your sake I will take every possible care."

The next day Funkum summoned Ngess to her office. She was a senior official and her summons had to be respected promptly. When Ngess got to her office, she smiled sweetly in welcome.

"Ngess," she said "Nyamfuka thinks the world about you. He is actually on his way here and says it was actually thanks to you that he managed to transform crude earth vehicle into something worth using."

Ngess feigned surprise.

"He is coming back already? That means he succeeded in transforming the earth vehicle. That young man is sharp."

"He certainly is," said Funkuin. Who would have been able to achieve such a complicated task so fast? I admit, he succeeded with your support, but the distance."

"That is good news," said Ngess meekly. "So, when is he arriving?"

"I don't know whether I should tell you that," replied Funkum. "You know he is still implicated in Fulumfuchong's conspiracy to destitute the king. I will need to clear him off first before anybody knows he is around."

"They still link him to the perfidy of Fulumfuchong?" asked Ngess with a touch of innocence on his face. Do you think Nyamfuka could have been that foolish to join such a reckless venture?"

"I trust my man," replied Funkuin. "He could not have been party to such a sordid plot?"

She eyed Ngess speculatively.

"Anyway, he wants to speak with you."

She called Nyamfuka and handed over the phone to Ngess.

"Hello!" said Ngess. "So our marooned citizen has managed to edge out of the virtually impossible situation?" he said this out loud for Funkuin to hear.

"Now listen," Nyamfuka whispered back "I hope you have made sure that Dr. Funkum is not eavesdropping."

"Go on," said Ngess.

"I will certainly be there in five days to make sure you are at the earth port." Nyamfuka whispered back. "You know I may certainly not have the opportunity of calling you again."

"It's OK, I have understood. Everything will be alright," said Ngess in a hurry as Funkum moved towards him.

To stop Nyamfuka to say anything foolish he continued.

"Have a good flight. Dr Funkum is a good woman and will certainly take care of you on arrival. I am sure you must be very lonely travelling all that distance alone."

"Hey," said Funkuin "I was already wondering whether there are earthlings with him. Since he is travelling all alone, there is no problem. A bit of loneliness will not kill him. It will rather make him to keep thinking about me."

Ngess handed over the phone. "Thank you doctor. I will go back to my lowly quarters now."

Ngess limped out.

18

Nyamfuka smiled with satisfaction as he analysed the message he had just received from Funkuin. He beckoned the captain who was leading the crack force that was accompanying him to Mungongoh

"Good news," he said. "The earth port in Mungongoh will be unguarded. From every indication the population shall be occupied with the ceremonious execution of the marines who had gone ahead with Fulumfuchong"

The captain grimaced "Is that the gruesome thing that is happening out there?"

"Yes. From every indication, before we get there, about fourteen of them would have been offered to the lions. Let's hope we get there in time to save the rest of them and Fulumfuchong."

"How are we going to operate when we get there? Demanded the captain

"Funkuin will be there to receive me. We will take her hostage till the operation is over. Make sure your men don't hurt her. Ngess will equally be there. He will take over from there and tell us what to do."

"But how shall we attack?" the captain was eager to know

"We don't have guns in Mungongoh. We have never known wars and obnoxious things like that since we settled in Mungongoh. We have concentrated all our knowledge on useful things and how to cope with an almost barren planet. Your men are trained fighters. I am sure we will simply need to fight our way to the king. When we destroy him and his close aides, everybody will rise in support of Fulumfuchong, you will see."

The landing in Mungongoh was smooth and without danger. Mungongoh had never known any attacking enemies. Neither had they ever received strangers or tourists. There was therefore no need for airport security and custom officials. At this specific moment when the king was personally presiding over the execution of the apprehended intruders, all flights had been suspended. There were no workers at the earth port apart from Ngess who emerged from an old hanger where he had been lurking. Just then Funkuin burst out from another hanger and sped towards the craft that had just landed. Watching her approach, Nyamfuka felt really sorry that this lovely lady was about to be embarrassed with the rough treatment that was awaiting her. Ngess himself was a bit embarrassed and withdrew to the cover of his hanger.

Nyamfuka descended from the craft accompanied by the squad. Funkuin rushed straight to Nyamfuka and fell on his chest, weeping with joy. Then suddenly she noticed the presence of the earthlings.

"Who are these?" she asked

"I am sorry," replied Nyamfuka, "but I need them to accomplish my mission."

"What mission?" she asked aggressively.

"I will explain later" replied Nyamfuka.

He turned to the soldiers. "Hold her prisoner but don't hurt her". He turned to Funkuin. "They will not hurt you. Just keep calm and everything will be fine."

Funkuin did not keep calm. She ranted, kicked, scratched and punched as the Americans lifted her off the ground and carried her into the craft where she was bound and gagged.

After the scene, which Ngess had been watching closely from the vantage point of his hangar, he emerged and strode towards Nyamfuka. Since Ngess was not of the class that

126

owned phones that could call across planets, he had made it a duty to be present at the Earth port for the past five days, given the fact that it was not possible for him to link up with Nyamfuka and find out exactly when the craft will arrive.

"Welcome back home," he said beaming at Nyamfuka. "The speed with which the earthlings constructed a copy of our space craft is proof that they are a force to recon with. Fulumfuchong is quite right that we should rather institute peace and cooperation with them than war"

"What is the situation now?" the anxious Nyamfuka asked. "How many Americans have perished in the jaws of the lions already?"

"This is already the seventh day since the gory entertainment started. Twelve of them have already been devoured. If we act fast, we might succeed in saving the two that have been programmed for today."

"Do you have any plan?" Nyamfuka asked.

"I have a simple strategy," replied Ngess, who had always known the right thing to do but was never listened to.

"By now the king would have come out of his palace and is moving in his royal coach to the amphitheatre of disaster. All the members of the IRDI are already there. I am sure Funkuin's absence will be conspicuous. I propose we move to the IRDI and grab the fast cars lined out there for official functions. Then, we use the side roads to get to the arena. If we act smartly we shall get there before the king. His coach moves slowly to give the pretentious tyrant the opportunity to smile and wave benignly at his people."

"What do we do when we get there?" asked Nyamfuka after translating the first part of the strategy to the captain and his men.

"We shall take cover not far from the royal entrance. You know that the conceited king Awobua has an entrance to himself, through which he moves straight to his podium. Once we are sure he has settled down, we will rush in, overpowering the royal guards on our way. We will burst in just when they are releasing the lions and send the king flying down into the arena. You know that in order to see and enjoy the gruesome spectacle best, the king's podium is located at a vantage point, not far off from the arena and with no possible obstacles. The chief minister and top brass although not on the same pedestal as the king, are close by. Your strong well built soldiers can easily toss him into the arena and thus divert the lions from the condemned men. We will then save the men and destroy a bad system. With those blokes gone, Mungongoh shall be free."

Nyamfuka thought it was an impeccable plan.

Ngess led them to the earth port car park where they occupied all the cars that were packed there. After briefly showing the earthlings how the things were driven, they all moved to the IRDI office where they switched vehicles for better performing ones.

Nyamfuka and Ngess concerted for a short while and agreed upon the side streets to use to get to the scene of the king's gory entertainment grounds. Since every citizen that was not eligible to occupy the limited spaces in the amphitheatre was required to throng along the main street through which the king would pass to get to the bloody ceremony, the other streets were quite devoid of people and easy to use. Nyamfuka and his men sped along and arrived at the amphitheatre discretely. They approached the amphitheatre from behind and parked around the entrance below that led into the cells where lions and condemned persons were kept. The area around the amphitheatre was clear and they could see the royal entrance at the far end. King Awobua was just driving in.

"You know the whole arrangement inside." continued Ngess. "Take thirty men and follow the door that leads to the king. He is well guarded but your soldiers are well trained and tough. Fight your way through to the king. You are aware of the fact that Mobuh and Itoff sit close by. "Don't spare them too"

Ngess looked round hastily "Now go and good luck."

"And you?" asked Nyamfuka

"I know the nether regions of this structure thoroughly well. I will take the rest of the men and go in there to where Fulumfuchong and Yivissi are incarcerated. It is also well guarded but we shall free them as well as the soldiers that are still alive and bring them back inside.

"Okay then," said Nyamfuka. "See you shortly."

The struggle to get to the king met with fierce resistance from royal guards with truncheons and it was difficult to get through. The well trained soldiers applied all the tricks and brute force possible. Karate chops and judo tactics were applied. Two marines of Japanese origin had come along with nunchakus and were putting them into good use. All the blunt objects that some of the soldiers had brought along, came in very handy. A similar struggle was going on in the basement where the cells were, and prisoners were kept. The surprised guards discovered that there were intruders when they were actually in front of the cells that held Fulumfuchong, Yivissi and the rest of the American soldiers. While the marines were warding off the guards Ngess released the prisoners. As Ngess herded Fulumfuchong and Yivissi towards the entrance, the released marines joined the others in the fight to subdue the ferocious Mungongoh guards.

Inside the amphitheatre, the American marines had worked their way to the king. Before he could realize it, the king was lifted from his seat and sent flying into the arena. Nyamfuka assisted three other marines in doing the same to Mobuh and Itoff. As they landed in the arena, the smart marines that had been placed in there as the day's treat to the lions used them as spring board to skip up to the podium of the arena and scale over. The metallic grill that held back the lions had just been raised for them to come out and feast. When the lion tenders discovered to their horror that their king and senior officials were rather the ones in the arena, they lost all composure and reasoning and rushed to block the lions. The lions knocked them down and went ahead to tear up their flesh. With the gates widely open and no body to close them, other hungry lions charged out. The flabby Mobuh attracted the lions most. Three of them rushed towards him and as he shrieked in fright, the forth lion made a beeline for the destitute king. King Awobua stood facing the oncoming lion as if he were Samson, capable of slaying the ferocious beast and harvesting honey from it later on. The relatively skinny Itoff ran to a far off wall and started struggling to climb. The smoothness of the wall however, thwarted all his efforts and he remained exposed to danger. Suddenly, he noticed one of the lions moving towards him. It had probably discovered that it could have a whole prey to itself instead of struggling with two other lions for Mobuh. Itoff's scream was sharper than the rest and almost frightened off the lion. It however overcame its hesitation and went for its feast.

19

Fulumfuchong was led into the amphitheatre through the royal entrance by Ngess. The sordid looking but very pretty Yivissi was by his side. All eyes of the frightened Mungongoh citizens in the amphitheatre settled on him as he moved to the king's seat. He pointed at Mobuh's seat and invited Ngess to occupy it. After a brief hesitation, Ngess jumped into it. Then, he picked up the sceptre that king Awobua had dropped in a hurry and sat in the king's chair. He beckoned Yivissi and placed her on his laps. He now turned to the waiting Nyamfuka.

"Let everybody have a seat. Meanwhile go and bring Dr Funkuin and place her on the seat previously occupied by Itoff."

After this last order, Fulumfuchong sat comfortably, with his sweetheart on his laps, to enjoy the spectacle in the arena. The destitute Awobua and his lieutenants were having a taste of their own medicine. Their faces were inert and disfigured by the claws of the lions that were now concentrating on their feast. The gory scene was quite captivating and nobody seemed to have noticed when Funkuin was brought in and installed in Itoff's seat. The feasting continued in the arena.

"Bring in more lions" ordered Fulumfuchong. I want those carcasses to be cleared off. Ten more lions were let in and within an hour there was virtually nothing left. But lions are messy eaters. If the people of Mungongoh had known about Hyenas, they would have reared them too and used them for cleaning up the mess left behind by the lions. Fulumfuchong picked up the cap of the dead king and placed it on his head. The cap too could transmit the king's messages better than any microphone.

"People of Mungongoh," he said. "As you have seen, nothing much has changed. You still have your king, your chief minister and your head of the IRID, only this time around the persons occupying these posts are more suited for them"

Fuinkuin was not sure that she had heard well. She was actually sitting in Itoff's seat but had still not come to terms with the reality.

"Your king now is Fulumfuchong, my chief Minister is Ngess and the head of the IRDI is Funkuin. The response from the floor showed that the applause for Awobua had been stage managed and artificial. The eruptions of mount Pelé and Krakatua put together would not have produced so much noise. The difference here was that the noise was joyous and happy.

Fulumfuchong waited patiently until the noise subsided

"The little change that I want to announce here," he continued "would be the position of a queen" he pointed at Yivissi. "From now on a new seat will always be placed by my side for the queen. I will not have to carry her on my laps every time we have an occasion. That should be reserved for our bedroom." Another joyous uproar made him to pause for a while. When it subsided he continued

"The queen is special, and this will become a most important position in Mungongoh." Fulumfuchong beamed round as everything he said seemed to be just what the people of Mungongoh had been waiting for all along.

"And now," he said. "We shall have something new. We all recognize the effort made by the earthlings to rid us of a tyrant king. We see from every indication that the earthlings are a force to reckon with and so an aggressive attitude towards them might rather land Mungongoh in trouble. On the other hand, cooperation with them can bring all the nice things on earth that Awobua had been lusting for, right to our door step here in Mungongoh. We could have regular flights to the earth instead of going there furtively as spies and enemies. For the sake of peace and cooperation therefore, we will have what the earthlings call an ambassador, only with us he will reside here in Mungongoh and not out there on earth. He will however make regular trips on earth to strengthen friendship ties, carry out trade negotiations and enhance cultural exchanges."

The new king turned to Nyamfuka

"Nyamfuka step out let them see you."

Nyamfuka glowed with pride as he stepped out.

"As earlier stated," concluded the new king, "Our policy towards the earth has changed completely. We must thank the President of America for the assistance he gave us in attaining freedom from Awobua. Specifically, we are grateful to these brave soldiers who accepted to follow me to a place unknown to them I wish to inform them that they are now honorary citizens of Mungongoh. But then, they are soldiers and have to go back and continue serving their country. What we shall do then is to give them some of our stones and pebbles which they cherish so much on earth. You won't believe me but earthlings are capable of killing one another just for a handful of these stones which we consider here in Mungongoh as rubbish. I think we shall allow each soldier to take back as much as he wants. That will equally show the earthlings out there that we are a force to reckon with."

The new king smiled at Yivissi.

"I believe we should show real gratitude to these soldiers," he said. "Don't you think so?"

"Certainly my dear," replied Yivissi. "We should also think of the families of the martyrs or the soldiers that were eaten by the lions. We should package some of the stones and send to them."

That is a very good idea," said the king. "Only a woman would have thought of that."

He turned to Ngess. "What do you think Ngess?"

"I think it is alright to reward the American boys sir," replied Ngess. "And the best reward in this case would be the shiny pebbles of Mungongoh as you mentioned. I also think it is a noble idea to think of the ones that lost their lives to lions. However, I have a small doubt as to the outcome."

"You think it may end up badly if we allowed them to go with what we consider as rubbish out here?" the king asked in surprise.

"You did not quite understand me sir," said Ngess. "My only problem is the greed inherent in every earthling. If you allow them to take as much as the want, each soldier would want to cart away tons of the stuff. Transportation would be a problem. Give them the stones, but measure out the quantities for each soldier. As for sending back some of these pebbles to the families of the slain soldiers, we can only do that through these soldiers here. But then, we should make them swear to hand over the packages intact. We have to guard against the possibility of their turning funny on arrival on earth because greed can provoke them to divert the packages destined for these bereaved families. My last worry is this idea of letting the greedy warmongers of the earth to know that Mungongoh is covered with what they consider as treasure. The mere thought of it would push the earthlings into all kinds of efforts to get to Mungongoh and help themselves with our rocks and pebbles."

"That makes one to shiver," said Yivissi.

"A reverse action to Mungongoh's previous intentions," said Nyamfuka. "Instead of conquering and taking over the earth, they rather invade Mungongoh and possibly make us slaves."

"Ngess is simply expressing a far-fetched fear," said Fulumfuchong. "When we go into mutual understandings with the earthlings, things like that would not occur. We are more advanced than them in many things and we are well protected."